...of John Brindley

'There is...
suspense,...

'clever, pacy and provocative stuff, set in an unforgettably lurid world.' *Daily Telegraph*

'strongly shaped by conflict between good and evil' *Bookseller*

RHINO BOY

'psychological horror at its best. Brindley's richly-imaged writing fairly burns with violence' *The Times*

'A tense and often dramatic story with some nice touches of humour' *Books for Keeps*

— · —

LEGEND

JOHN BRINDLEY

CHAPTER HEAD ILLUSTRATIONS BY
Ian P. Benfold Haywood

Orion
Children's Books

First published in Great Britain in 2009
by Orion Children's Books
a division of the Orion Publishing Group Ltd
Orion House
5 Upper St Martin's Lane
London WC2H 9EA
An Hachette UK Company

1 3 5 7 9 10 8 6 4 2

A catalogue record for this book
is available from the British Library

ISBN 978 1 84255 7181

Typeset by Input Data Services Ltd, Bridgwater, Somerset

Printed in Great Britain by Clays Ltd, St Ives plc

www.orionbooks.co.uk
www.johnbrindley.co.uk

This book is dedicated to Vanessa –
my very good friend

PART ONE

The
Underworld

One

Blake Newton – England's Olympic Future!

The day after Blake's best-ever race, the headline shouted out all over the place.

'Junior Champion smashes former 200m record!'

There it was, still on the wall two years later, along with all the other newspaper cuttings his dad had pinned up in Blake's bedroom.

'Under-17s champion sprinter beats record running time by massive margin!'

He'd taken more than half a second off the record, which may not sound a lot, but over that distance it was what his headteacher had called, speaking to the whole school, a phenomenal achievement.

All that was not so long ago; but it felt as if it had happened in another life. Especially looking back at it from here and now, when all the changes in his body had come, bringing – what had they brought? His age had made him suddenly broader, stronger and more powerful – yes, but also less flexible, heavier, slower. So what had that period in Blake's quickly developing life done for him?

'Blake!' his dad was shouting, thudding by outside his door. 'Are you ready? You're going to be late – and so am I!'

He could not even make the qualifying times for the Nationals, now that he'd gone from the Under-17s to the Under-19s. He wasn't anywhere near the mark!

'Blake!' With a massive single thump at the door. 'I'm off to work. I need to know you're ready for school.'

School! Blake was supposed to be at sixth-form college, doing his sports science. He was supposed to be involved in National Athletics. He was not supposed to be doing exam re-sits and plodding away down at the running club in the local park trying to keep his weight down and being treated like – like a failure!

His dad was still shouting at him: 'Blake – you're going on that school trip, right? Get moving!'

School trips to medical research centres! Studying biology, maths – re-sitting GCSEs, like an idiot, like a failure!

That was all he was now. What had he done, he asked himself, staring at the wall full of newspaper cuttings, to deserve having everything taken away from him like this? What was he now?

'I'm nothing,' he whispered, reaching out, ripping one of the pages from the wall. 'A big fat zero!'

'Blake!' His dad was rapping on the door again. 'What's wrong with you?'

'Nothing!' Blake called back, tearing the newspapers down, one after the other.

And then, so quickly, it was finished. They were all gone. Blake looked down at the pieces of torn paper littering his bed as the door blasted open and his dad came in.

'Hurry up, I said ... What's this? What's going on?'

'Nothing,' he said again, pushing by, going out of the room and down the stairs before his dad could say anything more.

'What have you done?' his dad was saying as Blake went for the stairs. 'You've spoiled it all – after everything you've achieved.'

But he was out of the front door and down the street before his dad could even begin to come out with it again: 'Blake, if your mother could see you now ... '

He'd begged his father not to say that any more. When he was winning races it was good. But now – not now!

Two

'What's up with you today?' Alfie asked on the coach.

Blake had been staring sullenly out of the window all the way, gazing at the houses giving way to farmland on the edge of the Great Western Moor. 'I'm just – finished, you know?' Blake said. 'Just – finished!'

The truth was he'd had enough of everything, and maybe even Alfie. They'd been friends since infants' school, but Blake had always suspected that Alfie liked him more than he liked Alfie. He could be funny sometimes, but then, once Blake had been around Alfie for a while, and the same-old, same-old gags came round again, the smile on Blake's face grew heavier and heavier. It was impossible to talk to Alfie about anything, when nothing was taken seriously enough to be worth talking about. But he was the only mate he had left who wasn't openly gladdened by Blake's failure.

'I know what you mean,' Alfie said.

'It's all this,' Blake said, waving his hand expansively, encompassing everything and everybody on the coach.

'Yeah,' Alfie agreed. 'Listen! Can you hear them, that little crew back there?'

The little crew Alfie was eavesdropping on were those involved in the chattering conversations. Blake was surrounded by A-Level students now. His old classmates had all moved onto the next stage in their lives.

Immediately behind, Blake could hear Vanessa talking.

Partially deaf, suffering from some kind of muscle-wasting disease that Blake could never remember the name of, she always spoke too loudly. Alfie liked doing his Vanessa voice, looking cross-eyed at Blake and trying to make him laugh again.

Like now, turning and kneeling on the seat next to Blake to peer over the back at Vanessa. 'And do you know the really, really interesting thing about mitochondria,' he said, interrupting the conversation behind, mimicking their earnest, serious tone, 'it was probably an independent organism in its own right, before it became incorporated into living cells as an organelle.'

'Yes,' Blake heard Vanessa's enthusiasm, 'imagine that. The part of our cells that supplies our energy was in a way a kind of creature itself once. Isn't that fascinating!'

'Indeed —' Alfie glanced at Blake '– simply fascinating!' He collapsed laughing next to Blake. 'Simply fascinating, eh, Blake, my good fellow?'

Blake's smile was stretched and heavy. 'Simply fascinating,' he repeated Alfie's words sourly.

He glanced again and again at Alfie. That stuff he had just recited from memory as a joke was about the body's energy systems, the way in which the cells supplied energy to be used by the muscles. Blake recognised it. It sounded right, too, for all he could tell. It was what Blake should have learned, but hadn't.

Alfie had, though. He remembered it, word-perfect. Neither of them had passed their biology exams but, Blake suspected, he had failed more thoroughly than Alfie. Blake, behind his false smile, was failing at everything more thoroughly than anyone.

Three

'Wow!' Alfie was pointing past Blake out of the window as the coach came to a halt at the security fences outside the grounds of the laboratories. 'It's like a prison camp. Blake, look – he's got a gun!'

Everyone on the coach knew that the labs had been surrounded by Animal Rights groups and that the research staff had been threatened with violence. It was in the paper sometimes, or on the news. They had all been told about it before the trip.

Blake hardly saw or heard anything of the tour, trudging round the blank white laboratories of the research centre, wishing he *could* care about biology. Cells and organelles and mitochondria and adenoside-triphosphate – he knew he'd have to understand it all one day, but every time he heard words like those, his mind would blur and make his head feel heavy. It was like listening to people babbling away in another language and trying to understand what they were saying.

Their tour guide, a surprisingly young-looking scientist, leading them through the labs between test tubes and microscopes, was speaking that other language right now. Blake was trailing behind, lumbering along with Alfie as the A-Level lovers took notes and peered at everything with serious and stern looks.

Alfie was walking with a limp the same as Vanessa's, wearing one of his MP3 earphones, like her with her hearing aid. He pretended to look into one of the microscopes but went too close and knocked his face on the eyepiece.

Congenital Muscular Dystrophy, Blake remembered, wasn't anything to laugh at, but when Alfie did that, hitting himself in the eye, stumping away on two unequal legs – Blake just couldn't help himself.

Separated by unsmiling teachers, with Blake on one side of the group and Alfie on the other, the tour guide was trying to engage the more unruly elements in the class by speaking directly to them. She started to tell Alfie about modifying mouse genes in the lab, until his cross-eyed concentrated stare made her switch her focus onto Blake.

'We do this,' she told him, 'to enable the study of human diseases under clinical conditions.'

Blake glanced over as Alfie said, 'So you mean to say that you modify the DNA of the mouse so that its proteins build cells shaped more like human cells?'

Only it wasn't Alfie speaking. It was Vanessa, with Alfie mimicking her from across the room.

'Yes,' the thin girl in the green lab coat and glasses turned and said to the girl in the green blazer and glasses. 'Yes, so that we can study the polio virus for example, under clinical conditions and—'

'So,' Vanessa interrupted.

Blake had to look away as Alfie was mouthing Vanessa's words with her, still miming her intense, almost frightened expression.

'So,' Alfie seemed to mouth with Vanessa, 'you make a mouse with human genes so that you can give it polio?'

Blake risked another glance at Alfie, who was staring cross-eyed at the lab assistant.

'Well,' the girl in the green lab coat said, 'not exactly. We use human DNA to slightly alter the mouse genes. But the mice develop in exactly the way they would ordinarily. Here,' she said, moving away, much to Blake's relief, 'come into the next lab. Let me show you.'

Blake followed her through, trying not to look at Alfie again, gazing round the walls of the next laboratory at the mice and rabbits and guinea-pigs in cages at the far end. Through a door between the cages, he could hear a monkey crying out.

Alfie was still peering about with Vanessa's concerned and serious expression. Blake had to look away, watching as the lab assistant held up a struggling grey mouse by its tail. She lowered it into her palm, allowing it to scamper from hand to hand. 'As you can see,' she smiled at Blake, 'the mouse is not altered or disturbed in any way.'

'Until you give it polio,' Blake heard Vanessa say.

'Or muscular dystrophy,' said Alfie.

Blake noted Vanessa glaring through her glasses at Alfie as the lab assistant placed the mouse into a little tank with glass sides. 'Muscular dystrophy, yes,' she said, flicking a switch. A tiny treadmill started up. The mouse was running along as if in its own miniature gym. 'All kinds of muscular diseases and congenital conditions are studied here. This,' she said, opening a locked refrigerator with a key from the bunch in her lab coat pocket, 'is one of our latest developments.'

She had trouble attracting Blake's and everyone else's attention from the little mouse having his work-out.

'This is what we are calling our mitochondria serum,' she said loudly. 'It's a very special device. It's not a drug, exactly. This is cutting-edge nano-technology in action. This serum contains billions of tiny energy conversion units capable of – well, let me show you.'

Blake's attention, along with everyone else's, was drawn now to the other mouse that the lab scientist took from a separate container.

'This,' she announced, with great relish and deliberation, 'is rather special. This is Supermouse.'

Four

Everyone's eyes were fixed on the super-rodent as she placed it on the treadmill next to what appeared to be its twin. Side by side they scuttled over the moving surface of the wide conveyor belt.

'Now,' the young scientist said, 'you will see what happens when I do this.' And her hand went to a dial fixed into the lab bench. As she turned it, the belt began to speed up. The legs of both mice kept pace, moving under them in a blur. 'Nothing unusual in that,' she said, as if to herself. 'But now, when I do this . . . ' And she flipped the dial fully round and the belt of the treadmill responded, speeding up and up until the first mouse collapsed in a little heap and was thrown back into the sawdust at the end of the conveyor.

Blake listened to the laughter erupting all round him. But his face was straight now. He was too busy studying the other mouse, the second one, Supermouse.

'Wow!' Alfie exclaimed. 'Look at it go!'

The scientist smiled now. 'And it will not tire, almost never. Not now that the serum has implanted many, many nano-technological synthetic mitochondria organelles into its every muscle cell. This mouse,' she beamed, pointing at the frantic, tireless rodent, 'is, at the moment, the fastest in the whole world.'

Five

Blake glanced at the serum in the young scientist's hand as the loser mouse flipped backwards again into a powder-puff of fine sawdust.

'Let me show you how it all works,' the guide was saying, starting to speak in her foreign language again, with a fat marker busy squeaking over a whiteboard.

But Blake was transfixed. He couldn't take his eyes from the rodent's little legs as they skittered across the still speeding treadmill, moving faster than sight, with the other mouse trying to climb back on the belt. It fell, pushed away again. But Supermouse was running like a champion, a super-sprinter, untiring and unbeatable. Blake felt proud that something, anything, could run so fast, the fastest in the world.

He tried to get a proper look into its face, to try to see how tired it was getting. But the mouse seemed so unconcerned, looking this way and that, as if this was just a part of its everyday training regime.

Blake could not resist reaching in and replacing the other mouse on the wide band and watching it struggle to keep up for a few moments. Supermouse never once glanced at its competitor disappearing from the race and being flung back in another sawdust puff.

'Why are you doing this?' came a voice from Blake's side.

Vanessa was next to him, speaking too loudly as ever, straight into Blake's left ear. He did not know what to say to her. Blake was never interested in the science, in the way Vanessa and her friends were, but he was fascinated, enraptured by the incredible performance power of Supermouse.

Vanessa sounded impatient. She asked again, even more loudly: 'Why are you doing this?'

Blake looked at her, about to ask why she was shouting at him.

'Why?' the scientist answered, before Blake could speak. 'Well, if we can stabilise the serum, as soon as we can control the level of the mitochondrial organelle devices bombarding the cells, we can begin to counteract the effects to treat all manner of motor-unit diseases like – like, well, muscular dystrophy, as your friend said, and—'

'Oh, no!' Vanessa said, as if to say that Alfie was definitely not her friend. 'No you don't!'

Vanessa's face had whitened in anger. The very young lab assistant was looking nervous. The teachers were suddenly on edge.

Alfie was next to Blake in a moment. 'Here we go!' he hissed.

The tour guide was still trying to talk Vanessa down. 'In order to study many life-threatening diseases, it's necessary to—'

But Vanessa had her hand in the mouse tank, snatching the running rodent and clasping it in her cupped hands. 'And what will happen to this poor little thing, eh?' She was thrusting her hands into the scientist's face.

A teacher took Vanessa by one thin shoulder.

'No!' she screamed. 'What happens to this poor little thing?'

'Well . . . ' the scientist tried to answer.

'You can't control it, you said!' Vanessa blared at her. The two teachers tried to drag her away.

One of Vanessa's friends took the mouse from her and kept putting it back into the scientist's face.

'That means,' Vanessa was crying out, her small frame being dragged back by the teachers, 'that means that poor creature can't stop, doesn't it!'

'It doesn't want to stop!' Alfie called out, grinning, nudging Blake.

Vanessa was struggling. 'It means it'll keep going till its heart gives out because you can't stop it now you've started it, can you!

It means you've destroyed that poor animal's life and you'll go on and on destroying lives looking for ways to make yourself look good! Because you haven't got muscular dystrophy, have you! You haven't got anything! And this is how you—'

This was when the teachers had dragged Vanessa backwards out of the lab door. But all Vanessa's friends were protesting now.

Alfie was trying to drag Blake into the commotion. 'This is more like it,' he laughed. 'This is why we love these educational trips so much, eh? Free Supermouse! Free Supermouse!' he was chanting, as the students were being ushered towards the exit door by their teachers and the lab staff.

Blake was being shoved out with all the rest, but his eyes were fixed on the refrigerator, into which the young flustered scientist, having taken the mouse and dropped it back onto its running belt, had tossed the miracle serum. He had noticed, as he was being jostled through the door, how the fridge door had been left, invitingly and tantalisingly, unlocked.

Six

Outside, and it was pandemonium. Vanessa and her friends were determined not to be pushed back into the coach without a fight. 'There were monkeys in that back room!' they were protesting. 'What will happen to them?'

Alfie was malingering on the outer edge of the chaos, trying to stir it up every time it looked like calming even slightly. He was showing off to Blake mainly, looking round at him, winking, throwing him a quick grin.

But Blake's attention was fixed on one thing only.

'Monkeys!' Alfie was yelping. He was jumping up and down. 'Save the monkeys, someone!'

Alfie was doing his very best to whip Vanessa into near-hysterics, but all Blake seemed to be able to hear was the humming sound of the mouse treadmill stepping up, faster and faster. He couldn't stop thinking about that little bottle of stuff.

One of Vanessa's antivivisectionist mates had made a break for it, running towards the main entrance of the research building. Two security guards in blue combat trousers left their posts at the entrance and the emergency exit to intercept her. She was being manhandled back across the car park to the coach.

Blake's heart was beating wildly, as if he too had been slogging it out on a treadmill next to Supermouse. He'd have been thrown flying into the sawdust, without any serum in his system. But with it . . .

With it . . . what could he do? And if the stuff wasn't a drug, surely it wouldn't be detectable. How would anybody ever know, if an athlete were to take just a tiny bit, just enough to . . .

But the ruckus was beginning to die down now that the two bulked-up security guards had got involved. Blake watched them taking hold of Vanessa.

Once again he thought he heard the turning of the treadmill. And then he saw the door of the refrigerator being slammed shut and left unlocked.

His heart was thumping as he came forward, nudging Alfie on the way. 'You can't force her!' he went at the security guards.

'Blake!' one of the teachers tried to order him back.

'Don't let them!' Blake insisted.

'Resist! Resist!' cried Alfie, picking up on the game again.

Vanessa resumed her struggles. Some of the girls already forced into the bus leapt back out. Alfie was still shouting.

But Blake was fading away, sloping off towards the back of the coach. The guards and the teachers and lab staff all had their hands full.

Nobody but Alfie noticed him go. Blake looked back at him and put his finger to his lips. Alfie's puzzled expression tried to ask a question, but Blake too quickly disappeared, diving for the bushes on the other side, ducking down and creeping unseen to the now-unguarded emergency exit door at the back of the building.

Seven

Entering the building through the emergency exit door, Blake was not sure where he was. He stopped, listening out for any alarms. There were none. Most of the security, he realised with a quick smile, was concentrated round the prison-wire periphery of the grounds.

He ran up the concrete steps and through a corridor looking for the Supermouse lab. The place was quiet now, except for the odd yell or scream audible from the car park.

Everywhere was deserted. It was so silent that Blake managed to catch the faintest of sounds in the distance. He ran down the corridor and round a corner with his excited heart reacting as if to a much harder sprint. What Blake had heard was a rhythmic hum he recognised. He followed the direction of the sound and came through a doorway back into the lab with the tiny treadmill still revolving. Supermouse was at full pelt, its non-stop muscles tireless, its rapid-fire reactions every bit a match for the electric motor whirring away under the bench.

Blake grinned, turning from mighty-mouse to refrigerator. He took a deep, deep breath and pulled open the door.

Inside were lots of different mixtures, serums and potions lined up in racks in the cold like magic potions at the ready. But there was just one lying on its side where it had been hurriedly tossed in by a worried lab assistant, the agitated junior researcher under attack.

Blake reached in and took the precious mitochondria serum.

He stood, clasping the near-frozen phial in his hot sweaty hand.

But he had no time to stand and gloat. Blake had to get back to the coach, before he was missed. He turned, grasping the little bottle to his chest. Then he stalled.

Blake looked at the slim bottle of clear, viscous fluid in his hand. With a dose of super-serum inside him, working into the cells of his muscles, nobody would be able to beat him.

With this stuff, he couldn't help thinking, he'd be National Champion again. World Champion!

It was then that Blake thought he could hear a familiar voice. He looked once more at the serum. The voice was one he'd known all his life, repeating something so very, very familiar.

Eight

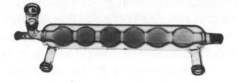

He was remembering that first time, well over two years ago, when he had won the two-hundred-metre sprint at national level. Blake remembered the tears in his father's eyes. 'Your mum would be so proud of you now,' he had said.

'I wish she was here,' the younger, swifter Blake had whispered.

'Oh, she can see you,' his father said. 'Don't worry, she can see what you're doing.'

And now Blake blinked down at the non-drug in his hand with which he was going to become a cheat. 'What *are* you doing?' he said to himself. 'Just what are you playing at?'

Shaking his head, as if to expel the madness, Blake turned again, stepping back towards the open refrigerator.

But before he had taken two steps, a door slammed just outside the laboratory. Blake heard voices. The scientists were on their way back.

He leapt over to the fridge and threw in the serum, slamming the door shut. From there, the only place he had to run was to the back of the lab and out through the other door. Glancing behind, he noticed that the refrigerator had swung open again.

No time to go back and close it. The footsteps of the lab staff were right outside. If he were to be found here now, with the fridge open like that, Blake knew he'd be in big, big trouble.

He moved quickly into the room beyond the lab.

As soon as he entered they started up. The odd animal cough and scratch that had emanated from this room turned into screech and wail as the inhabitants of a hundred, two hundred or more cages clutched at the bars and thumped at the sides to get his attention. Hundreds of hungry creatures looked his way, with tiny monkey-hands reaching through the bars, small dogs whining, cats spitting and rabbits thumping. Enough mice for a town infestation were scrabbling at the glass sides of their tanks.

'Shh!' Blake hissed, automatically reaching for the open hand of a really cute monkey peering at him with wide, hungry eyes. 'Be quiet! Please be – OW!'

The monkey had gripped Blake's hand and pulled it close enough to the bars to give him a nip on the finger.

'OW!' he shouted, too loud.

All the animals responded with shouts and screams and cries of their own.

Blake ran between the cages, between the clutching claws towards the dark rear of the room. There was another door and Blake dragged it open and plunged through.

He found himself in some kind of food store. The walls were lined with fruit, shelves stacked with nuts and vegetables. There was even a glass-topped freezer full of fish, Blake noticed, as he looked for another way out.

There were two other doors. The first one he tried was locked. Through a little narrow window, Blake saw that it led to what appeared to be a dimly lit staircase. The other door had no handle to pull, just a button next to it. The doors slid open as soon as he pressed it and Blake leapt into a little lift, tripping over some kind of trolley.

There was only one button to press inside. Blake shuffled impatiently as the slow doors closed. He waited, somehow expecting the lift to rise.

It fell. Blake felt himself being lowered, down and down. He looked for some indication as to which floor he was being taken to. There was nothing. The lift just continued to drop.

'Come on, come *on*!' He clenched his teeth. 'How far down can it go?'

The elevator was either moving very slowly, or they were sinking into some kind of deep basement. And by the feel of it, he was falling really quite quickly.

Then it jolted to a halt. Blake held his breath for the few moments before the doors began to open again. For all he knew, he was about to be exposed to a room full of expectant, heavily armed security guards.

But there was nothing. The sliding doors thumped wide to show just that – nothing. Outside, all was in darkness, as if the lift had stopped in the middle of a nothingness that went on falling away, into the very centre of the earth.

Nine

Lights came on automatically, illuminating a long corridor as the elevator doors closed behind Blake's back. The walls were blank, no doors, no windows, disappearing into the far dark distance.

'What *is* this place?' whispered Blake.

From behind him, the sound of the lift as it began its long ascent. Someone above had pressed the button. They were still coming for him.

Blake had no choice. This corridor had to lead somewhere. He had to find a way out, to get back to the coach before it started off without him.

He had to run.

Blake's head went down and he sprinted. His mum would have been proud of him, once. Now he did not want to disgrace her memory.

Up ahead, darkness. But then more lights, showing another far, far distance. Two hundred, four hundred metres came and went.

His lungs were bursting. Blake wasn't built to run this far. He felt sick, with worry as well as with the effort. The corridor did not end. It seemed as if it never would, his legs heavy as if wading through wet concrete.

The lift was coming down again, he knew it. There was nowhere to hide. He had to get to the end. He had to get out.

Then, at last, the final set of flickering lights were igniting to show the double exit doors at the end of the race and Blake was flying through with hands just barely in front of lowered head. To Blake's relief, there were no security guards, but he hadn't time to wonder why. He threw himself at the release handles and the doors crashed wide.

Blake fell out into the cold fresh air. He saw the hills surrounding him and the low winter sun as he collapsed against the armoured metal plates covering the closed double doors behind.

Blake went down as a wolf-pack of huge slavering dogs flew at his face. The heat of their breath hit him like a slap of warm dead meat. Thick, smelly slobber like rabid drool spattered across Blake's mouth.

The dogs were colossal, dark-haired and mangy, with rough, matted fur through which the blue-mauve of thick, sore-scabbed skin showed. They were on him, left and right, razor-snapping as he dragged himself harder against the doors.

Blake cried out. His voice was drowned by the hyena-like howls from six starving open mouths full of curved yellow fangs and quivering violet, violent tongues. He shoved back and back, reaching behind for the handles. But there were none on this side of the door. There was no escape.

The barking howls of the dogs were growing ever more hysterical as Blake's face came back out from behind his protective arm. The dripping, clamping mouths, three to his left and three right, were horribly close, but they were not quite able to get at him. The dogs were tethered, on chains just long enough to keep them away – only just.

Not all of them were tethered though, just one either side, with a thick studded collar round its neck. But they all struggled and raged to break free, as if one collar was enough to hold back three flailing heads. Blake leaned over to see how this was being done.

He cried out in terror. This time, his voice carried. This time, with the fear and horror of what he saw, he shouted even louder than they barked – even over the three roaring heads left and three right, with their one left and one right body.

Ten

From somewhere only slightly further away, Blake's terrified cry was echoed back at him as if from everywhere at once, but magnified and made more bestial.

At his back, the doors had slammed closed. Blake could not return. Instead, he drove forward, diving through the gap between the two triple-faced furious monsters. There was just enough room to thrust forward with so many red-raw fanged gums and blood-stained teeth gnashing at him. He plunged through the narrow space, falling head-over-heels, jumping up to turn and get a better look.

Now he could see the creatures properly, he felt even more horrified by the wide hair-tufted shoulders supporting the three heads each. These exit doors were guarded by monsters, all gnashing at him, restrained only by the length and the strength of the thick chains. The two outside heads on each body kept trying to turn, to snap at the central one for holding them back.

A huge blur of red fur was in his face, roaring at him. He fell back, very nearly into the snap and crunch limits of the dogs raging behind him.

The colossal beast-body in front jumped into the air with its long fur flying. Blake turned and ran, but a whole tribe of screaming mad devil-creatures leapt after him.

He turned the other way. Behind him, the shrieks sounded like laughter from kill-crazed sub-humans. Blake dashed away from the sound.

Ahead were assorted buildings, little brick huts and houses, like some kind of stunted village. Blake sprinted up the street.

More dark devils, all shapes and sizes, were loping out of the buildings as if they haunted these houses. Rolling at his heels, snapping for his ankles, Blake found himself staring into the strangest of pale, almost white eyes.

Blake ran even harder.

'Here!' a voice called to him.

'Where?' He ducked, shouting, surrounded by distortions, by terror, by chatter and dreadful laughter.

Some other kind of dog-like thing came along, walking on two legs, looking left and right, attached to white-and-brown scuttling things on leads.

'Where are you?' Blake cried out.

'Here! Over here!'

Blake saw an arm, a dark-skinned human hand waving him over from across the street. He tried to dash past the approaching nightmare of distorted demons stalking him, but they tugged at his trouser-legs and Blake went down in a heap. In an instant they were all over him, their little tight claws clutching at his clothes.

From the corner of his eye Blake saw the knives they carried, the sharp steel blades glinting with malevolence in the half-light. He scrambled away, as a rain of wooden splinters fell bouncing and scattering in the road.

Blake managed to scramble across the street, falling into the little house from where the girl's voice had been calling to him. He dived inside and slammed closed the door.

The dark-skinned girl inside stood very close to him as he breathed and shook. Her hand came up as if to touch his cheek. 'I saw you were so afraid,' she said.

Blake turned away and took a peek round the door. 'They're all still out there!' he said, shoving the door closed again. It seemed to have no latch or lock. The terrible tribes outside had gathered, peering over with bleached-white eyes, with strange dog-sighs, with call-cries against the swaying red fur of the monster in their midst.

'They'll break in!' Blake turned to the girl.

'Who will?' she asked.

Blake took a longer look at her dark and very pretty face. She was quite small, with skin that shone, or shimmered with almost rainbow colours in the low light. '*They* will!' he said, urgently. 'The mad things out there!'

The girl obviously did not know what danger she was in. 'Mad?' she said. 'Why mad?'

He looked more closely at her. The girl was staring at him through the biggest, blackest eyes Blake had ever seen. When she blinked, her eyelashes swept with such force, Blake thought he could feel the movement of the displaced air.

'You're not one of them,' she said then, as Blake looked at his own shocked features reflected in the endless depths of those eyes. 'I saw you were different, straightaway. Who are you?' she asked.

'I – I'm Blake,' he said.

'Blake?' And her features changed. The girl's eyes widened still further in surprise. Pleasure spread across her pretty face, stretching the skin.

It was not until that moment that Blake noticed the girl had no hair. The lashes of her eyes and the dark pools of her massive irises had transfixed him. But now he saw her more fully, following the stretch of the skin away from the pleasure expressed in her face, past two of the tiniest ears, to a completely smooth and shining head.

'Blake!' she was saying to him. She seemed to struggle for a moment, as if trying to get closer to him while being held back. 'Is it really you?' She beamed.

As she struggled again, Blake felt himself moving away from her, his back pressing harder against the door.

'Are you really Blake?'

He nodded.

'But I love you!' she said, beaming at him.

Eleven

'What?' he stammered. 'What? You – what?'

'I do – I love what you've written,' she said, her face withdrawing from Blake's shock and surprise. 'I've read it so much,' she said, turning from him to look about for something.

Now Blake saw her – as she turned, as she slapped her hands on the wooden floor, as she flipped away. 'But!' he was still stammering. 'But you – you're – you're!'

Blake was pointing at the girl's body in sheer horror.

She was looking down at herself, at the place where her legs would have been, had she possessed any. She, and Blake, examined her sleek, lithe, black, shiny body, all the way down to her splayed tail.

Blake dashed from her to the other side of the room. 'What are you?' he said, pointing at her in fear. 'You – you look like some kind of seal! Or some kind of – mermaid!'

Twelve

'Mermaid?' she asked.

Blake tried to back further away. But there was nowhere else to go. The mermaid-seal-girl was between him and the door.

'I have these books,' she was saying.

Blake looked past her at a tangle of weird and terrible creatures gathered like misrepresentations of reality in the dead gloom, peering in and chattering and screeching and baring spiteful white teeth. 'Away from me!' he roared in terror through the open doorway. 'Stay away from me!'

'But what's wrong?' the mer-monstrous girl was asking as Blake collapsed in the far corner with his arms over his head.

'Let me go!' Blake cried, as convinced now as when the two triple dogs' heads had been barking in his face, that he was about to be torn to pieces. 'Stop them! Let me go!'

'Why aren't you wearing the Unseen Green?' Blake heard the girl asking him.

He looked up. She was pointing to the other wall at a couple of green lab coats, like the one the tour guide had been wearing.

'We've never seen anyone like you without one of those on,' said the girl.

'Let me go,' Blake said again.

'What's stopping you?' she asked.

From outside, the room was filled with dreadful laughter, made more bestial for emanating from open mouths filled with fangs and red-raw gums.

'Here!' she cried back at him, fear coming into her face now, as if she had caught it from Blake. 'Take this!' she said, flinging the lab coat at him. 'Unseen Green!'

Blake could not bear to watch her moving her body as she seal-slapped across the floor. He ran for the open door.

'Are you really Blake?' he heard her say, as he peered out.

The eyes outside sank back into the gloom of the further shadows. Here and there, a bare tooth flashed, or maybe a knife blade. 'They're all still out there,' he said, glancing back over his shoulder.

'Just keep the coat,' she said. 'But before you go – are you really him?'

But Blake did not bother to answer, slipping back out into the street, running away as quickly as he could from the eyes watching under cover of darkness, with his feet crunching over the little pieces of wood strewn all over the concrete pavements.

Thirteen

Blake charged through the street, turning the corner at the end, up another road and out into the fields. As he ran away, Blake glanced back at the strangest little village ever built, a gathering of miniature houses darkening quietly in the long shadows of the hills on the edge of the moor. It looked peaceful now, as if ordinary people lived there.

All round the village, positioned at intervals on chains, the dread dogs of triple-drool sat or lay asleep or awake or both at the same time. The two that had attacked Blake were over the other side of the village. Now he faced more, many more. The whole place was ringed by them. It had been a mistake to believe he could just walk away. Nothing could get by without being torn to pieces and eaten. And eaten and eaten.

As he crept closer, three heads came up simultaneously in triple horrifying unison. The low growling sounded like endless, insatiable hunger rumbling, fuelled by acid drool.

Blake stalled. He wanted to hide, holding just the green lab coat in front of him. It was made out of ordinary fibres, cotton or something like it, but it had an extraordinary effect. As soon as Blake held it up, the hunger-sounds stopped. He dropped it, and the rumble resumed.

Putting the coat on, Blake could not believe what happened. The dogs immediately looked away, or sat or lay back down, licking their paws or dropping into a doze.

It was as if, with the coat on, they could not see him.

He chanced a few steps closer.

They did not respond.

The Unseen Green!

Blake looked down at himself draped in the green lab coat. He pulled it more closely around him as he stepped inside the chain-length distance to the nearest dog.

A giant yawn showed Blake the depths of the raw-meat interior of one dog's throat. He had to imagine all three mouths leading to the one insatiable stomach, each head fighting to tear and do the eating for the three, to be the one to try to ease the constant ache of appetite.

Afraid and doubtful as he was, Blake had to put all his faith in the invisibility powers of his lab coat as he shuffled with shifting eyes between the dozing yawning lip-licking dogs. He hardly dared breathe until he was on the other side of the ring of dogs and safely separated from them by the length and the strength of their fetters.

Taking one last look back at the hamlet of horror nestling in the fold of the rolling hills, at the research labs looming on the far horizon, Blake turned and ran away. With the three-headed ring of dogs disappearing behind him, Blake ran for the barbed wire fencing which had to be the periphery of this place, the entrance to, or exit from, Hell.

Fourteen

All round the wire fencing, facing out into the further fields where sheep gently grazed, huge signs hung:

YOU ARE TRESPASSING!
GREAT DANGER!
GO BACK THE WAY YOU CAME!
MINISTRY OF DEFENCE PROPERTY

Figuring, from the signs, that he was now outside and free, Blake removed the Unseen Green coat. The moment the coat slid from his shoulders, the heads of the grazing sheep came up.

Then, as soon as they spotted him, they charged. Not one or two of them, but all. Every last one of them turned and looked, and lunged.

Blake suddenly found himself running from these other beasts with the green coat flapping in his hand. As they thundered closer, the sheep turned out to be much, much bigger than he'd thought. They *were* sheep, but nearly twice the normal size, with cruel curly horns that speared out from aggressive foreheads between fluffy white wool.

The sheep were stampeding towards him, heads down, thrusting horns first, thundering across the rough grass. Blake staggered in one direction then the other. The sheep came at him from everywhere. He dodged one, another, struggling to get at least one arm back into the sleeve of the Unseen Green.

It was no use. He stumbled in the tangled grass and

immediately felt himself butted hard from behind. Blake flew into the air, thumping down onto his back. The grass was thick and soft enough to break his fall.

Hitting and bouncing on the ground, Blake went into a spin and curled up in a ball waiting for the thud and pierce of sword-sharp horns. He tensed, but no blade-head battered against him as he crunched into the ground, tangled up in the green lab coat that had got wrapped around him.

Being very careful not to show too much of himself, he pulled the Unseen Green further over his body until he was able to stuff his arms back into the sleeves. Even as he stood, holding the coat closely to his body, not one sheep cast so much as a glance in his direction.

Still shaking, breathing heavily, Blake continued on his way, passing through the giant sheepfold, putting more and more distance between him and that vile village disappearing into the early evening dusk.

Blake's breath was blowing like smoke in the cold as he made it to another barbed wire fence with yet more signs:

PRIVATE PROPERTY
MINISTRY OF DEFENCE
WEAPONS TESTING
MILITARY MANOUEVRES
GREAT DANGER!
DO NOT ENTER!

Standing on the other side of the wire, Blake looked back across the fields through which he had passed. The sheepfold went all the way round the hamlet, judging by the way the wire curved away in both directions. If anyone went through the wire, they'd be chased back. Beyond the sheep, the triple-champing dogs-of-war slavered, half-starved.

Far off between the distant hills, there was a light. He headed for that. Over the spongy moorland grass he jogged, looking up every now and again at the lights that seemed to be drawing quickly towards him. Then he saw that what he was looking at was a line of cars moving along. From where he now was Blake could see a road sweeping down between the hills. It must be the one, he thought, that the coach had come down to get to the research centre. He wondered if it had gone back this way, or if they were all still waiting, looking for him back there.

He took off the lab coat and stuffed it under a rock. Then Blake started to run harder towards the road to meet the traffic. As he did not have a clue how far away he was from anywhere, he was going to need a lift to the nearest town.

As he ran he started to wave. The road and the cars were closer now. Blake could see that there were four vehicles, all white, driving very fast, all bunched together.

He waved at them again. As he did, their lights came on. Not their headlights, which were already ablaze, but the flashing lamps on the four car roofs, beaming out a blinking blue warning across the darkening grass.

Blake ran from the moor onto the road as the cars all skidded to a rollicking halt and eight armed policemen rushed out. Blake, about to run to them, faltered at the huge bodies striving forward to surround and confront him.

'Don't you move a muscle!' the head on the first huge and imposing body bellowed straight into Blake's face.

Fifteen

'What's this, then?' he heard a voice say. 'Look at it, boy!'

Blake eased open his eyes which he'd shut in terror. He didn't understand what he was seeing held there in front of him.

'What's this?' the policeman said, angrily forcing the thing closer, shoving it into Blake's face.

Blake was about to ask the policeman the same thing – what is it? All he knew was that he was staring at a bottle of fluid. Not the phial that the mitochondria serum had been in, but a proper medicine bottle with a red label.

'I – I ... ' Blake was stammering, as his arms were jammed behind his back and the dangerous-looking stuff was taken away, only to be replaced immediately by a police face every bit as red and angry as the medicine label had appeared.

'What's your name, boy?'

'Blake.'

'What's your *first* name?'

'That is my first name.'

'I wouldn't mess with me, lad, if I were you. What's your name – your first and your second name?'

'My name's Blake Newton.'

The policeman nodded, as if he already knew. 'Blake Newton,' he said, 'I am arresting you for stealing a very dangerous substance from the premises of the ... '

'But I haven't!'

'... from the premises of the Research Centre Laboratories. You have the right to remain silent ... '

'But I didn't take anything!'

'... anything you do say will be taken down and may be used in evidence against you.'

'But I never! I never took anything! Please,' Blake was nearly crying as they were pushing him into the back of one of the cars. 'Please believe me – I've never seen that bottle before now!'

Only when the door slammed in his face did Blake fall back and feel them – only then, as he felt the bite of the handcuffs locked round his wrists did he look up and see the other man standing alone next to one of the other vehicles in a dark blue business suit. He was staring at Blake with his face flickering, going on and off with the revolutions of the flashing blue light on the roof of the police car.

Sixteen

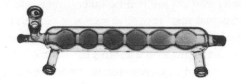

He was kept in a room for hours and hours. The police questioned him again and again. Blake told them the truth, but not all of it.

'I didn't take anything! I didn't! I told you, I ran out the back through the cages and went down in a lift into a long corridor. I went to a different place—'

'Blake! Blake!' the officer in the suit kept interrupting him. 'Of course you went to a different place. Do you know what that stuff is you stole?'

'But I didn't – I didn't!'

'It's a Class-A drug. You must have known that. How much did you take?'

'I didn't take anything!'

'I mean, how much did you swallow? How do you feel?'

'But I – please, please listen to me. I never saw that bottle until they showed it to me on the moor.'

'Do I need to get a doctor to look you over? Your eyes still look strange.'

Blake had been wiping away his tears of frustration and fear. 'I don't need a doctor. I need my dad. Call my dad, please.'

'Oh, we have, son. He knows what kind of trouble you're in, don't worry.'

As soon as Blake saw his dad's face, with worry piled on worry written there, he knew he'd never get the whole truth out.

'Dad, I didn't do it. I ran away and I found this place where there were these big dogs and—'

'Don't!' his father would not listen. 'Don't you dare!'

'But, Dad!'

'Blake – I've seen it. They have you on film.'

'Film?'

'Of course, you idiot fool! I've seen it. I've seen what you did – sneaking back into that place, taking that stuff out of the fridge. It's all there, Blake, for everyone to see.'

They were staring at each other. 'But if – if they filmed me taking it—'

'So you did take it!'

'No! I mean – Dad, I didn't.'

'Then why did you say you did?'

'It was a different stuff. For running – mitochondria serum – not a drug. I wanted it so much – Dad, I'm sorry!'

Tears were running down his father's face.

'Dad, if they filmed me taking it, they must be able to show me putting it back.'

But his father's head was shaking in disbelief and exasperation.

'Dad. I couldn't do it. I couldn't – I thought of Mum . . . '

But Blake's father turned away from him, taking a deep breath, shaking with emotion. 'Thought of your mum? If you had, if you'd thought of her, or me, you wouldn't have gone back in there at all, would you?'

Blake turned away. He couldn't bear to see the look in his father's eyes, the dark despair of total disappointment. It looked like fear.

It made Blake feel afraid, and all alone, as if he himself had been transfigured and sat, slavering by his father's side, with three heads and a bloodied, ever-starving open mouth.

Seventeen

The solicitor didn't get to the police station to arrange bail until after half-past eight in the morning. Blake and his father were there all night. Most of that time they said nothing to each other.

Driving home, his dad sustained the silence. It was almost too much for Blake to bear, the rage of no voices, the nothing-more-to-be-said between them, reinforcing the accusations and Blake's guilt.

'They must have planted that bottle on me,' Blake tried to say at one point.

'I don't want to hear about it!' his dad snapped, almost shouting, gripping the steering wheel hard.

His dad had noticed the slit torn in the sleeve of Blake's jacket.

'The dogs did it – the ones I told you about.'

'No! I *told* you, I don't want to hear any more about that rubbish. Stop it!'

At home, the raging silence was even worse. Blake had to sit in the kitchen and eat some cereal that tasted like wet cardboard in his mouth. His dad made two mugs of tea, setting one down next to Blake's breakfast bowl without a word.

Blake wanted to say sorry again. He tried to look into his father's eyes, but his dad avoided looking at him.

'Get some sleep,' he told Blake, speaking too quietly, walking away into the other room.

Before getting into bed, Blake could hear his father on the

phone making an excuse to take the day off work. 'I have a blinding headache.'

It was probably true. His father did get really bad headaches. Now Blake had one too. He lay in bed with his eyes thumping, the cardboard cereal in his stomach setting hard. Every time he closed his eyes he saw himself, as if on camera, sneaking like a thief into the laboratory.

Opening his eyes, he felt his breath being taken away. He lay gasping, as if he had only just run the length of that long blank corridor.

He crashed through the bathroom door exactly as he had through the double exit doors into the nightmare of the distorted dogs barking in his face, their acid spit in his mouth.

Blake retched over the toilet bowl. He staggered to the sink and rinsed his mouth and face. Looking up into the bathroom mirror, immediately behind his own pale features hung his father's worried expression.

'I am sorry, Dad,' Blake said, to the reflection.

Again his father shook his head in disbelief. 'Get it all out of your system,' he said.

Back in bed, Blake turned in the cold, in a sweat, in a shiver. He rolled over and over, tied into his tangled sheets, kicking them away, curling up on the mattress. He'd been awake all night. He was more tired than he'd ever been. But to close his eyes again meant seeing himself too clearly, as if on the film he had never watched. He saw himself taking the mitochondria serum out, looking at it in the palm of his hand. But the bottle was much bigger now, with a livid red label.

On the film playing behind Blake's eyes, nothing was returned to its rightful place, no bottle in his hand left unopened, or unsampled. In a tangle of damp blanket he watched himself putting substances in his mouth, turning to look up at the camera with a wild and beastlike look in his eyes.

Blake was running. He had grown three heads, his eyes were stark white, his teeth fang-like and dripping. In this version of events he ran down the corridor with his wild hair flying, snorting and stamping, roaring through the double doors as the scientists working over their lab benches looked up from their microscopes in horror. In a whirl of sweat and drooling saliva, Blake stamped and turned, wrapped in his own drugged flesh until his father caught him by the shoulder and shook him hard.

His dad was looking down at Blake in his bed. 'Get up, son. It's time to go to school.'

'School?' Blake was gasping, glancing at his bedside clock, as his dad was walking out of the room. 'But it's nearly the afternoon, isn't it?'

'It doesn't matter,' his dad said, without looking back. 'Get dressed.'

Eighteen

Mrs Gordon, the head, was waiting for them in the corridor. She ushered them straight into her office and sat father and son next to each other in front of her desk. 'Now,' she said, without once glancing in Blake's direction, 'I'm not going to say anything about what has happened – other than the fact that we are all very, very disappointed.'

Blake looked away as the head teacher shared a long, sympathetic look with his father.

'He's on film,' his father said, breaking the Head's long silence. 'They have a film of my son ... and all he can do is come to me with stories of running underground into another place, some other world guarded by dogs with three heads!'

Mrs Gordon gave Blake's dad a kindly half-smile. She nodded. 'I understand,' she said.

Blake shot an urgent look at her.

'It's Greek mythology,' she said, still without looking at him, concentrating instead on his father. 'The three-headed dog Cerberus was the gigantic hound that guarded the gates of Hades – the Underworld.'

'Cerberus?' Blake heard his father repeating.

'Yes. In Greek mythology Cerberus guards the gates of Hades, or Hell, kept there to prevent ghosts from leaving the Underworld. Blake has obviously come across these stories – in class, perhaps? Possibly. But they do tend to stick in the mind – in the subconscious mind. And then, in the presence of – let's say – certain stimulants . . .'

'I see,' Blake's father was nodding by his side. 'I see.'

He didn't. Nobody but Blake saw the dogs, or smelled their hot savage breath or felt the acid burn of their drooling bark. Only he had run up the darkening street with a nightmare distortion of twisted creatures snapping at his heels to a house where a mermaid had lain in wait for him . . .

'Blake?'

He seemed to come to, brought back again from that other world, the Underworld, to find his head teacher saying his name.

'Blake? How are you feeling now?'

'OK,' he said. He lied, of course. Maybe he'd never feel OK again, for the rest of his life.

'In which case,' Mrs Gordon smiled again at Blake's father, 'I think all we should do is try to return to normal. The authorities will take all the necessary action.'

And she paused, almost as if to allow Blake to think again about the actions that may be brought against him.

'Blake has to report to the police station Monday, Wednesday and Friday, after school, every week until the court case,' his father said, as if answering some kind of question that the Head had not asked.

'And today's Friday,' she nodded. 'So, I think Blake should try not to miss any more classes, don't you?'

Blake didn't answer. He left it to his dad, who must have nodded. Blake couldn't see him, concentrating, as he was, on the images of Hades, the Underworld, that he seemed to see in Mrs Gordon's carpet.

Nineteen

Even before he came back, the seating positions had been changed, moving Blake away from Alfie.

Now Blake sat on the edge of his chair by himself. Everyone else was concentrating fiercely on the teacher at the front, or on their maths books, all trying not to look over at Blake. He crouched, alone and tensed, with a head full of Hades, the gateway to Hell.

After the lesson, at the end of the short school day, Alfie caught up with him as Blake hurried out through the crowded corridors.

'You all right?' Alfie sidled up to him.

'Yeah,' Blake said, without looking round at his friend. 'I'm all right.'

There was a long pause. They made their way out of the building together. 'You know what I thought,' Alfie said eventually, 'I thought you were going back into that place to get that other gear – the Supermouse serum.'

Blake paused. He managed to turn and look at Alfie. 'What? Why else would I have been going back in there?'

Alfie stopped too, but said nothing.

'I'm late,' Blake said. 'I've got to go.' He turned away.

'The police came round,' Alfie said, suddenly, halting Blake again. 'To my house.'

Blake took a step closer. 'And what did you say to them?'

'Nothing. They wanted to know if you'd ever taken – had – anything, before, like.'

'Had?'

'Yeah. They told my mum you were a ... They told her you stole loads of drugs.'

'And you believed them?'

Alfie shrugged. 'Me? No. But my mum – you know. Anyway, they're the police. Why would they lie?'

Twenty

Running through the streets, overdue for his appointment at the police station, Blake felt as if he was still charging through the half-light of dusk in the nightmare hamlet in the hills, with vicious creatures snarling at him all the way. He ran into the police building, expecting more threats and attacks.

But the duty officer asked him if he was all right, noticing how flushed and agitated he was. Blake had to sign his name and print the date on a registration form as policemen came in and went out, taking no notice of him.

Blake's conversation with Alfie kept coming back to him, as if Alfie were asking him over and over why the police would lie.

'Lad?' a man's voice came at him. 'Have you done it?'

Blake came to, realising that he'd been standing over the registration book just staring, recollecting a face; not the angry features of the raging cop who'd apparently discovered the big red bottle in his jacket on the moor, but the other expression, the satisfaction on the features of the blue-suited man standing back, flickering on and off in the false blue police emergency light.

'Yes, I'm done,' Blake said, straightening. 'Can I go now?'

The policeman nodded, giving Blake a wink. 'See you here on Monday. Don't forget!'

By the exit door, two more policemen moved aside to let Blake through. But they stood very close to the door, watching Blake as he stepped out onto the concrete stairs down to the street.

'Blake Newton?' a man said, as a camera flashed again and

again. 'Are you Blake Newton, the former British sprint champion?'

The camera kept going, catching every faltering step that Blake took away from the police station.

'Is your name Blake Newton?'

Blake glanced back at the faces wavering in the doorway behind him.

'Are you the national championship runner? We're from the Eclipse Newspaper Group. Can we have a few words?'

'Yes,' he said, his every movement punctuated by another flash. 'What do you want to speak to me about?'

'About your running, of course,' the reporter smiled.

Blake took a last glance at the police faces behind the closed glass door. Only now there were more of them, six or seven gathered there in a bunch.

'We're interested in you as a national junior running champion. Would you mind if I asked you a few questions?'

'Like what?' Blake said warily.

'Like,' the newspaper man said, 'did your parents know you were taking illegal substances when you were winning your races?'

Twenty-One

Blake had never seen his father so mad, barely able to control himself. He'd stormed out into the night, leaving Blake alone in the house, still trying to convince someone of the truth – still trying to convince himself.

Later, as Blake lay in bed, too frightened to close his eyes, he heard his father downstairs. He'd come back after the pubs had closed. Blake could hear glasses clinking, or bottles. Over the sound of the TV, he heard his father stumble and mutter.

Blake's dad never drank. Not since those first few weeks after Blake's mother's funeral. His dad had stayed drunk all that time, so drunk that Blake had begun to think that he'd never pull himself together again.

It lasted until his dad found Blake crying, saying, 'I don't want them to put me into care, Dad. I don't want them to take me away.'

Blake would never forget the look on his dad's face then, at the moment of recognition as to what he had been doing to his only son. The next day, they had rowed a boat together, down the River Moor through the Great Western Moor to the estuary town of Moormouth – a trip of triple Moors, as his mum had called it, that they had made once before. Blake remembered his mum, sitting in the back of the boat while he and his dad took it in turns to row gently downstream. That other day, with just the two of them back in the boat, his dad had looked at Blake with that expression still on his face. 'Your mum loved this river,' he said, 'and the moor, and all the little towns and villages. I can still feel her, here with us, now – can't you, Blake? She can still see us. I'm not going to let her, or you, down.'

He felt as if he were already missing his dad, as if a wedge had been driven between them. He was thinking about all the things they did together, watching football, rowing boats, even off-road driving sometimes.

But now, downstairs, with the frosty morning casting a low white light through the window, Blake's dad's sleeping, hung-over face still seemed to carry that look of disappointment. Of pain. His face was too pale. He'd probably need to be sick when he woke.

Blake, careful not to disturb him, crammed some dry bread into his mouth and washed it down with milk. He gathered his running kit together and put it in his bag.

It was Saturday morning. The sun was still just peeking over the rooftops. Blake had hardly slept, but he didn't feel tired. His head was spinning, his hands twitching with the energy of nervous tension. He needed to train, to run as hard as he could. Feeling this way, sparking and jumping, he might just make those qualifying times after all. It would be ironic if that were to happen, now. And it would be such a shame that his dad would not be there to see him.

Twenty-Two

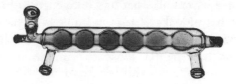

It was too early yet for the athletics club. Blake had to walk round the almost empty streets, keeping a careful eye out for anyone looking like a newspaper or TV reporter with a cameraman over their shoulder.

As he passed by, someone came out of one of the houses, a man appearing very suddenly. Blake leapt, as if it were some kind of moorland distortion loping towards him, but the man didn't notice Blake standing there shaking. He just walked quickly up the street looking at his wristwatch.

In the white, sparkling park, with the frosty grass snapping under his trainers, Blake watched the dog walkers – more ordinary people, with everyday pets, animals on leads, or let loose to run for a stick. An excited boxer ran past him with a line of drool swinging from its flattened chops. Blake flinched, but the dog carried on by, blundering along on all fours, with just the one head to tell it which way to go.

The world was as it had always been. The frost was real, melting in the rising sun. People walked about unaffected by legends, tales of the Underworld, unafraid of ghosts or horror stories.

Where had he been, really? Blake had to question himself – was it as he remembered, in actuality? The park and the people and the early birds flying would suggest to him that he was the one who had got it all wrong.

But then if that were so, had he, in reality, stolen something, some other, more hallucinatory substance from that fridge? And if he had, could he have tasted some of it? He'd never have done that – except, perhaps, by accident?

Now, as he made his way to a cafe for a cup of hot tea, Blake could not properly recall what had happened to him. Once he had opened that unlocked fridge, once he had reached into the cold containing the serums and the drugs, what kind of hallucinations had he let loose to run amok through his mind?

At school last year, they had learned about the effects of drugs, the harm done and the hallucinatory tricks played on the mind. How was it possible to discern the truth like that? Drinking his tea in the steaming cafe, Blake still felt disoriented, confused, out of touch with reality.

Whatever the whole truth was, he decided, walking to the running club, he alone had snuck back into the lab with every intention of stealing from that fridge. The fault was his. He was going to have to face the trouble he was in, running to confront it as quickly as he possibly could.

His sprint trainer, Jimmy, looked up from lacing his track shoes the instant Blake appeared in the doorway of the changing rooms. He had a surprised, or more like shocked, look on his face. Jimmy straightened, breathing in deeply. Another couple of lads, already there, stood behind him.

'Hi, Jim,' Blake said, trying to sound as natural and calm as he could.

'Blake,' Jimmy said. 'I wasn't expecting – what are you doing here this morning?'

The other boys looked away from Blake as he glanced at each of them. Blake went to speak, but his voice failed him. The look on Jimmy's face was already saying too much.

Still Jimmy just looked at Blake, even as he reached to pick up what was lying on the changing room bench.

Blake and Jim were locked, eye to eye as Jimmy handed him what he had stretched for. Blake took it from him. It was the morning paper.

Jim nodded, indicating that Blake should take a look. Unfurled, the headline said it all:

Drugs Taint National Athletics —
At Junior Level!

Blake stood blinking at the big black words. Under the headlines, the questions:

'Do we need to drugs test our children?'

'Is no one safe from this threat?'

The threat the newspaper spoke of was Blake. He knew it. He looked up into Jimmy's threatened face.

'Can't do it, son,' Jim said. He gave a pitiful shake of his head. 'For all I know, you might still be—'

'Jim, I'm not. Believe me.'

'Can't risk it, son. Sorry. I'd have called your dad, if I'd realised he was still going to let you come this morning.'

'I have to run,' said Blake quietly, aware of the crowd gathering at his back.

'Run, then,' Jim said. 'But not here.'

'Jim, please. Please!'

'Blake, I can't have you here. Not now. I've got the club – I've got the others to think of. You have to go.'

The other boys looked away again as more arrived, stalling at the changing room door.

Tears were filling Blake's eyes. He dare not blink, or they would fall, cascading down his cheeks.

'Now, Blake, please,' Jimmy said. His mouth, his expression looked sorry, but his body language said that he was dead set, that what he was saying was the end.

From behind Blake they came, the other boys from the door, moving to arrange their kit bags on the benches, trying to behave as if nothing was happening. No one said anything.

No one, except Jimmy, looked at Blake. 'Please,' Jim said, even more firmly.

As he turned away, Blake blinked. With his eyes streaming, he ran out, watched by the boys gathered at the exit of their changing rooms, and by the girls crowding out of theirs.

Blake sprinted across the track and out of the gate back into the park. His footprints showed across the melting frost on the grass. He ran away, under the trees dripping in his face, diluting the salt water already running there.

Twenty-Three

Marching through the town centre with nowhere now to go and nothing to do, Blake kept his head down, with eyes fixed firmly to the ground. Outside the newsagent's, he had seen the board:

**Local Junior Running Hero
On Drugs Charge!**

Even now he tried to hide and failed. Too often he felt eyes alighting on the side of his face, identifying him, knowing about him, more than he knew about himself.

When he saw Vanessa in the shopping mall, Blake turned away quickly. He didn't think he could bear to suffer her judgemental expression amongst all the others, her against-everything campaigning eyes boring into him.

There she was, at this moment, as Blake glanced behind, handing out leaflets in front of the hamburger bar. She had not noticed him yet. Blake halted, hiding in a shop doorway, watching her.

Vanessa was with some people Blake did not know, not kids from school. One looked like she could have been Vanessa's mother. They had a placard saying, 'MEAT IS MURDER!'

The vegetarian society was out in force. Blake knew they'd never make a difference like this. People laughed at them. He and Alfie had, many times. But now he couldn't help but study Vanessa as she struggled to stop her head from going into that twitching fit she often did, as she limped along, offering out her leaflets. An old lady took one and Vanessa smiled, as if she had achieved something really worthwhile.

Blake watched as the busy shoppers shifted round her, ignoring or mocking her. One man yapped out an insult, an obscenely rude word. But eventually Vanessa was able to give away another leaflet with another smile. Blake watched Vanessa turn to share her feelings with the woman he was now convinced was her mother. Vanessa's mum's eyes shone as she looked at her daughter. Blake felt the warmth of the mother's smile. He had seen, had felt that self-same blaze from his father, and not only when Blake had done well on the track.

But Blake's father was probably still snoring in a stupor at home. And Blake was left stranded here, unable to do anything to change the situation he was in, staggering forward from his doorway with the realisation that he was envious of Vanessa.

There she was, limping along and trying not to twitch her head, while here he gasped, jealous that she had not done nor could do any wrong. In her mother's eyes, Vanessa was everything he wished to be again for his father.

And then, before he could prevent it, she had spotted him peering over at her. Vanessa had seen the look on Blake's face. He could see her reaction to it in the shift of emphasis in her expression. In a moment her initial appalled disgust was swept away. Vanessa's face changed in response to his.

She, limping and twitching, growing steadily worse year by year, took one look and her spite turned into pity.

She started to approach, not holding out her leaflets as before, but offering a thin, semi-transparent-skinned hand.

Blake turned and ran again, with nowhere to go but back to the wet park. As he dashed past, the runners warming up on the track in the athletics club stopped to watch him go. Blake was fast, but nowhere near fast enough. Everyone could still see him, and see him more clearly than he could himself.

But Blake ran. He dashed through the trees to the bridge over the river. There he halted, with his breath billowing like smoke, tears growing cold all over his face.

He looked down into the river's deep middle, the dark swirling current flowing constantly below him. Wiping the freezing tears from his face, he swung his kit open bag over the top and let it go. It looped slowly through the air, with track shoes and towel and shorts and sports vest falling out into the water before the bag splashed down further upstream.

Blake watched his stuff sink as it tumbled in the current. The running shoes quickly disappeared, but shorts and vest, sinking slowly, looked like him, as he was, the old Blake, the good runner, drowning.

His past life, all of it, was drifting away into the darkness under the bridge, never to appear again on the other side. He dropped to his knees, trying to disappear, to dissolve into the water falling from the bare branches covering his head with the hood from his jacket.

Two pieces of wood fell onto the pedestrian path nearby, as if from the watery trees. But then, Blake felt another, in his hair, *under* his hood.

He reached in for it. He picked up the other two. These were the things the little devils with knives had been throwing at him, as if in attack. Bits of wood had got lodged inside his hood.

Blake stood, looking more and more closely at them. They were not just ordinary sticks. These were little carvings, tiny effigies like miniature statues.

The more Blake studied them, the closer they drew in his concentration. These were the most intricate, delicately tiny carvings imaginable. And . . .

He almost staggered back.

One of them looked like . . .

No, two of them – all! Each was different from the others in many ways, but all were the same in one aspect. In all three, once he looked closely enough, he could see the same thing.

Each of the effigies bore the same face! And that face was, unmistakably – yes, it was! – his own.

Twenty-Four

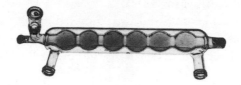

The little devils he'd thought were lunging at him with flashing blades had not been on the attack! Their knives weren't weapons, or else he'd have been cut, many times. There had been so many of them, he realised now, that had they assaulted him he'd never have made it out of the village.

Blake's hands shook with the three little figurines in them. What he held now could show his dad, and the world. This was proof – wasn't it? Proof that he had not done what they said – proof that he *had* been to the village, the weirdest, most frightening place in the world – proof that he *had* seen the dogs with three heads and the mermaid and all the other grim abominations.

Gateway to the Underworld or not, Blake did not know. But now he knew one thing for sure, the thing he had lost in all his confusion and doubt – that he was innocent.

Twenty-Five

His dad was breathing heavily over the kitchen sink when Blake burst in through the back door.

'Dad!'

His father's head came up. 'Jimmy called,' he said. 'He told me you went to the club.'

'Yeah,' said Blake. 'I did. But then—'

'Don't go anywhere!' His dad turned away, taking a drink from a glass of water.

Blake still stood by the sink clutching the wooden figurines. He waited while his dad sat heavily at the kitchen table with his shoulders sinking, his head resting against an open palm.

'Dad, it's really not what you think. I can show you.'

'What did *you* think?' His dad looked up. 'That Jimmy was going to accept you, as if nothing had happened? He told me about the headlines. Have you seen the papers?'

'Yeah. It doesn't matter, I've—'

'Doesn't matter!'

'No! I mean, it does. But there's something else. You've got to see this. Look!'

And Blake stepped over to lay his evidence out on the table top, three tiny wooden statuettes of him, with his own honest face looking up in triplicate at his bleary-eyed, white-faced father.

'Look closely,' Blake said, as his dad tried to focus. 'Look very closely at their faces. See? Can you see?'

His dad blinked a few more times. Blake heard him sigh. 'What's this supposed to be?'

'Look at their faces!' Blake almost shouted. 'It's me! See? *See?* It's me!'

Blake's dad glanced up at him with tired-looking eyes. He peered down again. 'Where did you get these?' he said.

'Dad, they're proof! They were stuck in the hood of my jacket. When I was in that place, that other place, there were these things with knives—'

'Knives?'

'Knives – lots of them. And I was surrounded by – by eyes and teeth and claws and there was this – this mermaid!'

'Oh. A mermaid.'

'Yeah. But the ones with the knives were all over me and I thought I was going to be cut but they'd made these tiny statues. Dad – they were giving them to me.'

Blake stopped. His father hadn't looked up again. 'Why didn't you tell me about the knives and the mermaids? Did you tell your head teacher about them?'

'No, I – you saw me on that film taking something out of that fridge. After that, no one was listening. Besides, there was only one mermaid,' Blake said. 'There were lots of other things hiding away so I couldn't see them properly – but only one – but only ...' Blake's speech was petering out against his dad's disbelief as their eyes met.

'Just the one ... mermaid,' Blake said, suddenly too aware of how he sounded right now, jabbering on and on as if any of this made sense.

'Jimmy saw you running through the park,' his dad said, when at last Blake's over-excited voice had died in his mouth. 'They all saw you running. They saw you throwing your kit into the river.'

'No, Dad, that doesn't matter now. You have to listen.'

'NO, SON! *You* have to listen!' Now Blake's dad was standing, staring into his son's face, studying him much, much harder than he had the wooden effigies. 'Don't you go thinking I'm drinking again,' his dad said, finally. 'I'm done with it now. That was just a – a moment of weakness. I'm strong now. I'm going to get you through this, Blake.'

'Get me through?'

'I'm stronger than that,' he said, glancing round, as if there was something over his shoulder threatening to overpower him. 'I'm here now,' he said, 'now you need help.'

But Blake was disturbed at the way his dad was staring at him, inspecting his eyes as if he did not trust them.

'You don't believe me,' Blake said.

'I believe you've got yourself into trouble,' he said. 'I believe my son needs my help.'

'But look at the figures, Dad! Look at their faces!'

'I've seen all the faces,' Blake's dad said, still staring at him. 'I've seen them all, Blake.'

'But you haven't!'

'Blake! You're not going out again.'

'Why?'

'You know why! You're in danger. These things you've been doing – when did it all start?'

Blake turned on his heels, squirming with disbelief and frustration. 'Dad! I don't – I can't – you're my dad!'

'Yes! That's why I'm keeping you here. Jimmy was going to call the police on you again. He thought you were going to do something stupid. He thought you needed protection.'

'But nothing happened. I went to the town.'

'Yes. Then you came back with these things!' And he flung out a hand, swiping the figures from the tabletop.

'Why can't you see what I can see?' Blake yelled.

'Because nobody can!' his dad shouted back at him. 'Nobody can see these monsters, these mermaids, Blake – only you.'

Twenty-Six

Waiting so long for his dad to go to bed, Blake fell asleep for a few moments. He bounced awake, fully dressed in bed.

When he glanced at his bedside clock, he saw that he hadn't just nodded off, but that hours had gone by and it was now almost three in the morning.

Blake crept out of bed, easing on his trainers. He tiptoed to the top of the stairs and stood there listening. Insomniac TV was all he heard, some ages-old film on for the thousandth time in the dead cold near-end of the night.

The bottom-but-one stair always creaked. Blake congratulated himself on remembering to step over it. He peeped through the open doorway.

There sat his dad. He was in the armchair and it was facing away from the television towards the open doorway. His dad had positioned himself like that, on guard, waiting to catch Blake doing exactly this – sneaking out. But he had fallen asleep, with his overtired eyes still weirdly half open, as if watching while unconscious, seeing, but unable to do anything about it.

At the front door, he halted. He shook his head and turned back. On the stairs, going back up, he forgot about the step which cracked and creaked like a loud alarm going off. Through the pounding in his head, because of his too-fiercely gritted teeth, Blake thought he could hear the rasp-bark of dogs growling into both ears and into his face all at the same time. He had to steady himself, holding hard onto the banister, waiting for ordinary late-night television to re-establish something like silence round him.

He continued back upstairs to his room, shaking the hounds out of his head. They'd been there all day, the other misshapen beasts of one form or another, white eyes and teeth, full fur flying, flashing blades, bald beautiful head and seal's tail.

She, most of all ... the mermaid ... because Blake could not rid himself of that image, that pretty face, the way she had said she loved him. She loved him, she said, and she'd been reading what he'd written.

What had he written?

Blake picked up his mobile phone. It was nearly new, not state-of-the-art or anything like it, but it's camera wasn't bad. At least it had lots of memory, with the card in it.

Back downstairs, hopping over the creaks near the bottom, he looked in on his dad once again. It still appeared as if he were trying to keep two half-eyes peeled to look out for his son as best he could.

Blake loved him, but his dad just didn't understand.

He would though, Blake was thinking, gripping his phone camera with nervous excitement, sliding out of the front door into the dark winter morning hours before the dawn, looking for a cab to take him at least part of the way back there.

Twenty-Seven

The hills of the moors clung onto the night as the sun threatened to show. Blake sat in the taxi for well over an hour to the little town on the edge of the Great Moor. From there, he had expected about another hour's walk over the grassy fields.

But it took a lot longer. It felt like hours and hours of stumbling through the darkness with images of monsters leaping out of his mind. Every new step he took shook his resolve. But he had to get his evidence. He had to find the Unseen Green lab coat he'd hidden under the stone if he was going to get near enough to take photos.

The sun was about to come up and Blake couldn't find the right place. Either that or the coat just wasn't there.

He came to the first line of razor wires with the EXTREME DANGER signs. Blake looked everywhere for the right stone. He found lots of stones, but no coat.

The sheep were there, on the other side, grazing peacefully. From here they didn't look any bigger or fiercer than ordinary sheep.

There was still no lab coat to be found. But if he could just get close enough, what more would he need than some pictures of three heads on one dog's body? With evidence, everyone would have to believe it, all of it, the dogs, the other monsters and the mermaid. That blue-suited man on the moor had fitted Blake up to hide the truth. Blake hadn't stolen anything – that was the truth. One good picture, maybe two, that was all he needed to start to prove his innocence to the one person who mattered most: his dad.

Blake scrambled under the wire, falling into the grass on his elbows and knees. Like the soldier in an army training film he'd seen, he snaked his way through, keeping his head and his backside down.

In a few minutes he was soaked through and very cold. But at the same time, he was sweating with the effort. Glancing back, he'd only covered a short distance, just a tiny fraction of the way. Every so often he had to take a peek around to be sure he wasn't about to run into any grazing or sleeping rams.

He lay gasping, trying to gather his strength. Although it was freezing cold and wet, Blake was glad that it was still mid-winter, with the dawn coming on so slowly. When he finally made it, scrambling under the next fence out of the grazing meadows, the moors were still largely unlit, with the sun just sparkling like a jewel between the distant hills.

Blake ran for it, tripping in the tangled undergrowth and falling, tumbling over and springing straight up. He ran until he could see the silent village resting ahead, with the research centre casting a long shadow further away on top of its hill in the early sunlight.

From between the rough moorland plants, Blake, lying on his stomach, peered down into the cleft in which the hamlet nestled. The little houses were still in darkness. It all looked like a ragged tear in the surface of the earth, an open rip into the Underworld that his head teacher had spoken of. From here, it did appear to be the entrance to the darkness, the depths from which every imaginable abomination could spill out into the ordinary world.

But its guardians, the fearful hounds of Hades itself, could not be seen from this distance. To get any valuable pictures, Blake was going to have to get a whole lot closer.

So again he scrambled like a soldier on military manoeuvres, fast now, as he was sliding downhill towards the open rend in the ground. Towards the darkness.

Keeping his head low, Blake ran to the first of the buildings. He tried to peep in through the glassless window, with his phone set on image capture. The dark interior of the hut showed nothing.

He stood on tiptoe and peered in. All was utter darkness. The camera was set to flash. He put it in the centre of the open window space and clicked, lighting up inside and flashing outside the hut.

It was then, at that moment, that he heard it.

Blake froze.

The low rumble of a hungry growl sounded close, too close to his left hand.

Then, to his right.

Behind him too, surrounding him in that sound.

He could smell their acid breath on the air. All round him, as if split back open by a single camera flash, the Underworld had sent its worst, its foulest stench, its lowest grumble-growl in three times three-fold, left, right, to Blake's centre, the very middle of his total terror.

Twenty-Eight

Nine heads roared at once, three brutal bodies thrusting forward at him. They pounced, mouths wide, teeth bared, ready to rip.

Blake leapt. His hand just managed to catch the bottom of the low roof of the little house. He heaved himself up, one foot catching on the bottom of the window through which he had been taking his picture.

His phone fell to the ground as the dogs drove forward, mouths smashing against the wall. Blake scrambled up, or tried to, with the huge hounds leaping, one catching him by the heel.

The sheer massive weight of the thing started to drag him back off the sloping roof. But the hold on his heel was not fast and the dog fell, its enraged faces disappearing as it floundered to the ground below.

Blake scratched to the top as the three dogs snapped nine-faced at the lowest edge of the roof. The air was wet with their bark-spit and battered by their sound. Blake, scrambling wildly to the top of the roof, overran the apex entirely and went sliding straight down the opposite slope. He dropped in a heap on the ground against the far side of the house.

Over he rolled and sprang up, dashing forward while the barks continued to rage on the other side. He ran along the road. But as he went, more roars sounded, with faces in threes appearing from round corners, from between the trees. Cerberus dogs, here and here were loping, heads down, shoulders hunched. A howl went up. Blake tried to run. A big black dog stepped out, its drooling mouths ever connected to starvation.

The brute crouched, ready to spring at him. Blake fell back. He turned. There was another. Another. They were everywhere now, running in, adding howl to roar, roar to howl. The street was slick with drool. Blake slid. He fell against the side of another house. Heat came at him, a breath-cloud he had to inhale as the dogs of death filled his every sense.

For an eternity the moment of crouch before pounce before crunch went on, collecting all Blake's fears and magnifying them infinitely into total terror. He fell back, crunched into the corner of wall and ground as rumble-growl turned to horror howl and the world was full to overflowing with fang in flight, a wall of open mouths flying in towards the epicentre that was Blake.

He might have screamed, there was no telling. The noise was too much, too loud and terrible. There was no sound loud enough to climb above it. Blake was contained in that sound for that moment as what he'd thought was the wall behind him gave way and he fell backwards.

One moment there was nothing but roar, the next and it was slam and crash and Blake was turning on his back in the spinning half-light, with a single window revolving over and above him.

Now he screamed. As the door through which he'd fallen closed, held in place by the colossal weight of a single body, Blake saw what horror looked over him now.

He crabbed backwards across the floor into the far corner as the mountainous red monster leaned its back against the door. Outside, the guard dogs of Hades raged, smashing their ivory fangs into the wood shutting them out. In here, across the little room, the long flowing fur of this next beast-thing shuddered with each slam. Its super-long arms were splayed, its huge flat feet spread out over the floor. Blake took a longer look at it. For the moment, the massive red primate-like man-monster was busy holding the door shut. But its eyes were fixed at where Blake crouched panting and ready to run, with nowhere to run: the room almost entirely full of deep-red fur and tiny blinking eyes and a grin-grimacing mouth threatening, promising, teeth – many, many more teeth.

Twenty-Nine

A shout from outside!

It sounded like a man, an ordinary person. Then a woman. Voices, raised but human – rescue!

Their voices rang out and the barking roars died down, disappearing into the distance.

But as soon as the thumping against the door subsided – before Blake could open his mouth to call for help – the closest creature was up and over him, bearing down on his corner, covering Blake in the longest, coarsest, thick hair. He struggled in a dense tangle, squashed against the two walls and the floor forming the corner into which he was being forced. Blake opened his mouth to call for help. He coughed, with his air passages invaded by hair, filled up so far he gagged and retched.

The weight bearing down on him just pressed harder and harder. Blake tried to cover his mouth and nose with his hands. He couldn't move. He coughed once more and the creature covering him coughed too.

Blake could hear the woman speaking quite close by. His own laboured breathing was too loud, his head wrapped in too much heavy hair to hear what was being said, other than the odd disconnected word. 'Noise,' he thought he heard. 'Today.'

'Nnng!' Blake was trying to call out.

'Hmmm!' The vast body pressed against him reverberated with the sound it was making.

No more dogs barked. Blake listened to a few more fuzzily broken sentences. Then all fell silent.

As the beast breathed, Blake's own space under it was constricted and released. He had to synchronise his inhalations and exhalations. Even then, he was going to be stifled to death under this pressure if it went on for very much longer.

Then, quite suddenly, the weight lifted from him. Air came flooding into his freed lungs, unimpaired by hair. It was so sweet to breathe, even though the air itself smelled of nothing but the beast. Blake could taste it, surprisingly perfumed and strong.

The huge thing turned on him. Its ferocious face came looming close, the white of its eyes not white, but light brown.

Blake, about to cry out again, found his mouth stopped by the brute's huge hand. It had clasped just about the whole of the bottom half of his face, peering very, very closely into his eyes.

'Shh!' it hissed at him, putting one of its fingers to its lips, like a child telling a friend to keep quiet.

It was a giant orang-utan, a red-brown primate with the longest and shiniest hair that Blake could imagine on any beast. The body of the creature seemed to flow as it moved, like rusty water swirling and eddying, coming to a standstill in ice patterns like frost on a window in the morning.

Gradually, as the huge ape kept its distance, Blake's breath started to settle. The way the thing kept looking out of the barely open door, glancing back at Blake, peeking out again, Blake began to believe that perhaps he was not about to be torn to pieces.

There were no dogs outside now, and no voices. The silence thickened around them in the little house. Blake found himself about to speak to the monstrous ape, before checking himself, holding harder onto his own arms, waiting for the right moment to run for the door.

But there would be no right moment. The beast was too big and too fast. Blake could not even begin to think to spring away from the wall before it loomed over him again, taking his arm in its dinner-plate-sized hand.

Blake cringed away, expecting after all to be dragged across the floor, to be trampled and broken up. But it didn't happen like that. The beast crouched, running both its hands down Blake's arms.

And there it sat, waiting, with Blake's face turned away in horror.

Blake felt its plastic-like hands firmly enfolding his. He turned his head to finally face the giant in front of him.

The ape bared its teeth.

Orang-utans didn't do that. Blake was trembling. Only human beings smiled, didn't they?

Blake's fear must have showed in his false smile back at the beast. As soon as Blake's face stretched out, the brute's true snarl came through. It wrenched Blake's arm almost from its socket, lifting him from the ground and pressing him to its chest.

Blake would still have cried out, he would have called for help, if only the wind wasn't being crushed out of him in the ape's clutches as it loped towards the door on the knuckles of its one free hand.

Thirty

Clouds moved over Blake's head, as if the great dome of the sky was spinning overhead. All the little buildings of the crazy village turned against the corner of his eye. Insane laughter cackled from all quarters. Blake was being swung violently as many hands made grabs for him. The strong arm constricting his lungs did not relent with its pressure, threatening to pop Blake's eyes from their sockets. From the chest against which his head was pressed, a rumble vibrated like thunder, augmenting into a roar.

The laughter rippled away into the distance as Blake's limp limbs were tossed in every direction. He was like a loose rag doll, with no strength left inside to kick or punch.

Under him, the fabric of the narrow road was replaced in an instant by rapid buildings, by speeding sky.

Another door was barged aside with a crash as the interior of another small house enfolded Blake's senses. He felt the arm at last relent its constant pressure.

As he fell back onto a wooden floor, the vision of the red ape's wide face veered into view, brown-eyed and bare toothed, just before it lifted away, accelerating astonishingly till it was a mere dot in the distance.

There it wavered for a moment. The hard air hit Blake's lungs and the ape-image disappeared completely, as if switched off.

Thirty-One

Blake found himself lying on his back looking up. He focused into the sheen of a very dark-skinned face. Blake was once again reminded how pretty she was, even without a single hair on her head.

'You!' he cried, scrambling up and back at the same time.

She exchanged a seal-glance with the red primate, who had returned. 'You've come back,' she said, at last.

Blake was breathing hard against the thump of his heart. He took a reassuring look in the direction of the red ape, who did not appear as if he were about to attack. From there, his eyes strayed to the beautiful black face, the perfectly rounded head, down the dark shining body to the heavy tail lying flat on the floor. 'What happened to you?' he said.

The strange girl blinked at Blake. Once again he was swept up in the motion of her eyelashes, in the round beauty of her deep black eyes. Only now did he notice that she was wearing something – not clothes exactly, but a black bikini-top. But only that, on an ice-cold morning in the middle of winter.

'Nothing happened,' she was saying, blinking, aiming a slow smile in Blake's direction. 'Not since your last visit. I was just hoping.'

Blake was swallowing his fear. He must have looked bemused.

'Hoping to see you,' she said. 'I wanted to get to see you again.'

It was then that Blake started to take note of her voice. He'd missed it in the excitement before now, but so strange it was that he could hardly tell now what she was saying. It was deep, so very deep. The sound seemed to come from way down inside her throat. Her lips barely moved, like a bad ventriloquist.

'Ridley agreed with me that you didn't belong here, that you weren't like all the others.' That sound rolled over him. 'But I thought you'd gone away and wouldn't come back.'

She seemed to be waiting for him to speak, eagerly anticipating the sound of Blake's voice. But he found himself unable to find anything to say. It felt all wrong for him, as if he were talking to a fish in bubbles of confused speech.

'But you did,' she said, giving him a smile.

Her teeth were tiny. Blake could see them all lined up in two very neat rows.

'Ridley?' he found himself saying.

The mer-girl glanced towards the wide, imposing presence of the orang-utan. 'Ridley.' She nodded, making a quick hand-signal to the ape before turning her attention back to Blake. 'Ridley said you were—'

'Ridley said?' Blake risked another glance into the expanse of the red-brown face stuck peering out impassively from the top of the huge primate body.

'Yes,' the girl said, with her head cocked just slightly in curiosity. 'Ridley told me that he thought you—'

'He – he told you? He can speak?'

'Yes, he can speak to me. Why not?'

Thirty-Two

'But he's a – he's an ape!'

Ridley gave a great primate grunt of prehistoric disapproval.

The top half of the mer-girl sent another hand signal to the red beast. He watched her, nodded and then signalled back.

'So he does speak to you?' Blake said.

'Of course!' She showed those two rows of tiny jewels lining her upper and lower jaws. 'Ridley speaks to everyone.'

Blake took a much longer look at Ridley, who, at the same time, sat regarding Blake, with his round, brown, intelligent eyes shifting and studying, closely observing everything.

'Does he,' Blake said nervously, 'does he shake hands?'

The girl smiled again. 'Yes, he shakes hands.' And she turned and made her signs at Ridley.

Blake was trying hard not to baulk, not to shy away back into his corner as Ridley's red-mountain body towered over him. The orang-utan's very, very long hand was extending towards Blake. This was not the first time Blake had held that hand, but shaking it now was different. The pressure Ridley exerted was measured, carefully, to be firm and warm and friendly.

Ridley let go of his hand, ever so gently. He made some signals in front of Blake.

Blake looked to the mer-girl. 'He's very pleased to make your acquaintance,' she said, nodding her approval.

Suddenly, Blake's head was swimming. He felt as if he were about to pass out again. The massive orang-utan was pleased to meet him, so a seal-girl said. 'I don't feel too good,' he said, holding his head between his legs.

Breathing, looking up again, he saw that the girl had shuffled closer to him, holding out a full cup. Blake took it and peered into its transparent surface.

'It's only water,' she smiled.

He drank, feeling better straight away. 'Does he,' Blake asked, 'does Ridley understand a smile?'

The girl nodded.

Ridley's grimace back at Blake was not so much a smile as just an exposure of teeth. But for an orang-utan, Blake had to suppose, it wasn't bad going.

'And you,' Blake turned to the girl, trying hard to concentrate on her face without looking at that terrible tail. He held out his hand to her. As she took it, Blake was surprised to find how cold she was.

'It's freezing in here,' he said. 'Shouldn't you be … ' And he tried to indicate just how little she was wearing.

'Freezing? Is it? It feels fine to me. I'm usually too hot. How are *you* feeling now?'

For the first time since his re-awakening, Blake halted to inspect himself for cuts and bruises or broken bones. He was surprised at what he found. 'I'm hungry,' he said. 'I'm starving!'

She smiled into his face. From behind him, Blake could still smell the strong sweet perfume emanating from Ridley. From the front, as if inhaled deeply, some other, very different aroma. 'I've got some food here,' the girl said.

Blake watched her slapping away across the floor to the other side of the room. Ridley was there, picking up a wooden ornament or statue. He held it out for Blake to see. It was a likeness of the girl, her face smiling, her sleek body, with the tail raised proudly. On the base of the statue, one word, beautifully carved: CHIMERA.

Blake took the statue from Ridley. 'Chime-era,' he read out.

The mermaid was slapping back towards him. 'No,' she said, 'it's pronounced Ky-mare-a.'

'That's your name?' Blake looked up.

'That's my name,' she said, holding something out to Blake.

73

It was a fish.

'I think it's thawed now,' she said.

Blake looked at it. 'Oh,' he said, looking about for the kitchen that could not possibly exist in the tiny square space inside what was not much more than a shed. 'Oh, I need somewhere to – cook it?'

The girl, Chimera, frowned. 'Cook it?' she said. 'Why don't you just ... ' and she tossed the whole raw fish into the air and caught it in her mouth.

Blake could see again those tiny teeth as they clamped onto the body of the fish. He watched with horrified surprise as Chimera, with a single flick of her head, turned the fish-head into her mouth. She lifted her face and allowed the whole thing to slide, head first, down her throat. For a few moments, Blake gasped to see her with just the tail sticking out of her mouth before finally swallowing the entire thing down. She looked at him, licking her lips, breathing her fish-fume breath straight into Blake's twitching nostrils.

Thirty-Three

'Oh,' she said, drawing away from the look of shocked horror Blake could not wipe quickly enough from his features. 'I thought you were like me. I thought you ate fish. Like the Greencoats say they do, although I've never seen them eat one.'

'I do eat fish,' said Blake, thinking of a slab of battered white flesh from the chippie, 'but not like that.'

'Oh,' said Chimera again, still responding to Blake's look of horror.

But Ridley suddenly crossed the room to the door in one smooth swing over his knuckles. He made his signs to Chimera, flicking his fingers, touching his lips. She nodded at him and he opened the door and loped out into the morning.

'What *is* this place?' Blake said.

'This place?' Chimera said, looking about. 'This is where I live.'

'Yes, but I mean – who are the Greencoats? Why are they—'

'Are you really Blake?' she interrupted him. It was as if his name had some secret power here, as if he himself were special.

He halted. 'What do you know about me?'

She reached for something. A book. 'Ridley says you're probably not Blake. But you say you are. I've read this,' she said, holding up a white book.

From where Blake stood, he could read the title: *Selected Poems of William Blake.*

'*Tyger, Tyger,*' the girl quoted.

Something stirred in Blake's memory. '*Burning bright,*' he said.

Her face lit up. '*Tyger, Tyger burning bright, in the forests of the night.*' She was beaming at him. 'The way you use words – your poetry, it's so unlike the way the Greencoats speak.'

'But I'm not . . . ' he started to say.

He stopped as the door flew aside with a crash. Tumbling through the opening came more village inhabitants – a gaggle of baboons, laughing hysterically. They ran up to Blake, leaping over him as he, overwhelmed by their numbers, shied away.

Blake turned and turned. The baboons, all laughing like children, tapped him on the shoulder or pinched his bottom. They tried to pull his trousers down.

'What's happening?' he shouted.

His voice was drowned out by the call-cries of the wild gang. 'Wha's happin?' they chattered between great gusts of maniac laughter.

Blake stared over at Chimera. 'Did they just say what I thought they said?'

Unable to hear him over the noise, she laughed and clapped her hands – no, she clapped her tail, slapping it down hard onto the bare wooden floor.

'Can they speak English?' Blake roared, with his arms out, laughing baboons hanging from them.

'Peek Ingliss?' the nearest to him were saying straight away.

'Peek Ingliss? Peek Ingliss?'

One flicked the buckle of Blake's belt and the others managed to tug down his jeans. 'Hey!' he cried.

Chimera's tail clapped harder. 'They don't understand what they're saying,' she laughed. 'But they know what they're doing!'

The baboon tribe shoved Blake from behind. As he went over, he was aware of a huge cow's head peering in sadly through the open window. 'Off me!' Blake was struggling underfoot on the floor, with his fear beginning to resurface. 'Off!'

'Off! Off! Off!'

The room was filled with baboon calls and laughter. 'Off!' they shouted out again and again.

Blake, looking up from the floor, saw several mouths at once, all laughing, chattering, mimicking words with their lips curled up. Their hands were all over him, plucking lightly at his clothing. They were rolling away, holding themselves against their side-splitting laughter.

If he struggled to get up, the hands tugged him back down. If he shouted out, they caught the cry and mimicked it.

'This is mad!'

'Mad! Mad! Mad!' they shrieked, with their sound growing, becoming so loud it felt as if the walls would blow out and the roof fall down.

Then, when the door smashed open again, it really did sound as if the place was about to explode. Ridley came in raging, flicking a long arm out, scooping up baboons one or two at a time and sending them spinning out of the door. They laughed and scampered, running round and round as Blake picked himself off the floor and pulled up his jeans.

As the last baboon was ejected, all that could be heard was Chimera's tail still slapping against the floorboards. 'The Boons!' she laughed. 'Only Ridley can control them. I don't know what we'd do without Ridley.'

Blake turned his attention to the giant orang-utan as Ridley held out his hand, the one he had not used to expel the Boons. The length of Ridley's hand looked to be about half Blake's arm. This one was full of fruit and nuts.

Ridley nodded at Blake to take the food. Blake did so gratefully.

'He said he thought you'd prefer his food,' Chimera smiled. 'And he was right. Ridley's nearly always right.'

As Blake ate the fruit, he watched Ridley swing over his knuckles into the corner of the room. From there, he picked up a hairbrush.

Blake looked towards totally bald Chimera. 'It's his brush,' she said. 'Ridley keeps hairbrushes everywhere.'

The orang-utan sprayed something onto his fur.

'And perfume,' Chimera said, as they watched the massive ape brushing his long red hair, looking at himself lovingly in a little hand-mirror.

Thirty-Four

The apple in Blake's mouth tasted the way the fruit always had, before today. The similarities with the outside confused Blake, almost as much as the differences. 'I don't understand,' he said, looking at his bitten apple, at Chimera's girl-face, at Ridley's perfumed hair-spray.

Ridley stopped brushing. He and Chimera were staring at Blake, two diverse faces bearing the same puzzled expression.

'What kind of place *is* this?' Blake asked.

The seal-girl and the orang-utan peered round the room, blinking. The cow's face reappeared in the window. It seemed to let out a great sigh, before moving away again.

'I mean,' Blake stammered, going to the window, 'I mean – so many things I've never seen, I've never even heard of before.' Outside, the cow was surrounded by tiny monkeys with little knives and pieces of wood.

'Like – out there!' Blake said. 'The little monkeys – they're making carvings, aren't they?'

'The Spiders – spider monkeys.'

'But they're making little models of the cow. And the cow – is it humming? It is, isn't it?'

'She's always got sad songs,' Chimera said, looking sorry too, as if in sympathy.

'But cows don't hum!'

'Don't they? Are you sure?'

But Blake was suddenly not sure of anything. He shook his

head. 'I've seen them, I've heard lots of them, and none of them ever—'

Both Chimera and Ridley seemed to jump at this news. 'You've seen lots of cows? Where?'

'All over the place. They don't hum, any of them! They just don't.'

'Do they sing, then?'

'No, they – they're just cows! Like – like you're all – I mean – I don't know what to make of this place. Dogs with three heads.'

Chimera laughed. She signed at Ridley. He clapped one hand against his forehead with his mouth open as if in silent laughter. 'They're not dogs,' Chimera smiled. 'They're Head Hounds.' She pointed through the gap where the door had swung open. 'There's a dog,' she said, as one passed by walking on two legs, glancing in for a moment before stalking away with its head in the air. It held a lead on the end of which a black and white rabbit scampered.

'This is a different world,' Blake said, peering through the open doorway, thinking about the place in Greek mythology his head teacher had talked about where Cerberus dogs stood guard. 'This is the Underworld!' he decided.

Chimera laughed again. Ridley's mouth came open. 'No – this is the Innerworld,' the mermaid said.

Then Ridley was pointing out a metal pole, on top of which were mounted a cluster of close-circuit TV cameras. But Blake was trying to take in all the details of this new world, this Innerworld where dogs walked rabbits and guinea-pig pets on leads and cows hummed tunes and tiny spider monkeys made art. Two white-eyed chimpanzees passed by, arm in arm.

'*Tyger, Tyger, burning bright,*' he could hear Chimera in the background, quoting. 'Tell me about that, Blake. *And what shoulder, and what art, could twist the sinews of thy heart.* Oh, tell me about that.'

Blake turned away from the door. 'First, tell me about the cameras up there. Who's watching – the Greencoats?'

Chimera nodded, simply, as if the answer were only too obvious, and too saddening.

'So they've seen me, then, have they?'

Ridley was brushing his hair again, looking in his mirror to ensure his parting was straight. He stopped to shake his head.

Chimera sat on her tail staring at Blake with her soft black eyes made very big. She took a quick glance at the orang-utan's shaking head. 'Ridley thinks they don't bother watching at night, when the Head Hounds are loose. There's nothing to see.'

'Why are they watching?'

'It's what they do. They watch, they write things down. I don't know what. But I'm sure it's nothing like your words, Blake. Tell me about that. Tell me about your poetry. Tell me about the Outerworld,' she was saying. 'Tell me what it's like, where you come from. Are there Greencoats everywhere? We thought there were, but there can't be, because you're not one of them. We knew that, as soon as we saw you, frightened of the Head Hounds. We knew you were different. Ridley said he didn't think you wanted to take any blood.'

'Take blood?'

'You – you don't, do you?'

'Blood? No. Why, do they? Doctors take blood for tests. What are the Greencoats looking for?'

But there came a crash from the roof. Ridley was up and out in a second, chasing the Boons down.

Chimera and Blake stood together peeking out of the half open door, watching Ridley chasing Boons up the street. Chimera laughed. Her voice, coming from deep within her throat, sounded like the return of an echo from a valley between the hills around the moor.

Blake couldn't resist another close look at her face. As he turned to her, she did the same to him. Blake saw himself again, reflected in the depths of those huge, soft eyes.

He heard her speak. 'Your world,' Chimera's eyes shone with deep inner light. 'It must be very wonderful. I've often felt there must be somewhere better than this, somewhere without boundaries or Head Hounds. I've dreamt of what it must be like to be there, to feel I'm where I belong.'

Blake could see the hope in her, the weight of the world she had built up through the poems of William Blake for him to live in and for her to wrap her dreams around. But the world wasn't up to her imaginings, he knew. There were hardly any tigers left to burn brightly anywhere, and William Blake was long dead, he was pretty sure. And he himself now lived in a spoilt place, a world made more and more intolerable by the accusations against him and the deterioration of his relationship with his father. The Outerworld, Blake's ordinary world, was not wonderful. Or if it ever had been, one look at Chimera ...

'One look at you,' he said, 'and my world was changed, for ever.'

Thirty-Five

Chimera held a hand to her mouth as if in fear. 'At me?' she said. 'What have I done?' Her every emotion, portrayed through her eyes and in her body language, appeared human.

'Nothing,' Blake said, looking more closely between her fingers as they touched her lips, at the fine web of skin connecting each to its neighbour. 'You haven't done anything,' he said, reaching out to take her hand, inspecting the black fingernails as thick and as pointed-sharp as claws. 'This is like nothing on earth,' he said. 'You are the only one – unique!'

'So are you,' she whispered. Her eyes were fixed open now, on Blake, taking him in, capturing him.

'You don't understand what I mean,' he said, still holding her hand, 'I'm not unusual, like you, something out of a legend. I came back to get some proof to show – or maybe to try to understand this place. But I'm just getting more and more confused. I have more questions now than before I returned.'

'But you have all the Outerworld! You can find out everything there, can't you? You are,' she said, turning those big black eyes away for a moment, 'the first person I've ever spoken to who can answer me in words. I love Ridley, but he could never talk to me in the way you do. I've listened to the Greencoats talking ever since I can remember. When I was little, in the other place—'

'You mean you weren't always here?'

'No, I was . . . somewhere different.'

'And what was that like?'

'It was loud, that's all I remember. Being scared. Being on my own. I was little there, when they used to make recordings of my sounds, trying to analyse them. My throat isn't like yours, Blake. I have to make speech sounds in a different way. The Greencoats gave up listening. I was trying to speak to them. But all they did was stick needles in me and inspect me and talk to each other as if I wasn't there, like they do now, as if I wasn't really alive, not like them.

'So I kept myself a secret. I found out quickly how cruel they were, my keepers. For a long time in that other place they kept hounds and lions, goats and snakes, and they killed most of them.'

'They killed them?'

'They only ever kept the biggest, the strongest and the fiercest. I thought they were going to kill me, Blake. I thought ... if I spoke, if they ever found out about me, they wouldn't like it, they wouldn't like me. But then I came here—'

'How?'

'I don't know. I was ... asleep. They put me out. I woke up here, with the dogs and the skinny pigs. And then Ridley came with the Boons. Then the Spiders. Then the others, then you, Blake, to talk to me in the words from my books.'

Blake watched as Chimera collected two slim volumes from the floor in the corner. She handed them to him. One was William Blake's *Selected Poems*. The other, a dictionary.

'I took them out of the pocket of an Unseen Green,' she said, most proudly. 'Ridley looks after them for me. I taught myself to read. I know all these words, except where some of the pages have fallen out. Nobody else here can do it. The Greencoats can. They can write. They do it all the time. But nobody reads for me,' she said, with hurt and regret. 'Nobody.'

Blake held the books in his hands. He opened the smaller of the two. He read out loud:

> '*To see a World in a Grain of Sand*
> *And a Heaven in a Wild Flower,*
> *Hold Infinity in the palm of your hand*
> *And Eternity in an hour.*'

He stopped reading. It was just a few lines. Blake didn't entirely understand what it was saying. He didn't have to. He looked up and saw what it said to her, to Chimera.

She was staring at him. Her eyes bigger, deeper than ever. She trembled slightly. 'I feel something for that, Blake,' she said. 'Your words, even when I don't fully understand them, they say so much.'

'I have to tell you, Chimera,' he said, about to confess to not being William Blake. He had to make it clear, because these words meant so much to her and he could feel her attachment to him through them.

'That's the first time you've used my name,' she said, with such a deep and dusky voice that touched Blake to feel the breadth of emotion she was experiencing.

'Chimera, I'm not . . . '

But the door blasted open at them and Ridley crashed through, signing urgently and glancing back desperately to the swinging door.

'They're coming for blood!' Chimera exclaimed, reading the great ape's arm and hand movements.

'Blood? Is it the Greencoats?'

Chimera's face was full of terror. 'It's always the Greencoats!' Chimera shifted away on her tail. 'They want blood – they're on their way here!'

Thirty-Six

Chimera's voice had altered. She let out a frightened wail, like that of a trapped animal.

Blake was crammed into the corner, hemmed in and hidden by Ridley's huge body. As he tensed to hear Chimera's expression of fear, he felt the orang-utan's every muscle flex. A low rumble of warning rolled up from Ridley's chest like an earthquake about to erupt.

'Just keep her still,' a man's voice said.

Ridley rumbled again, his back tensing and flexing with nervous electricity.

'Should we take out the orang?' another man's voice came to Blake next.

Then he could hear Chimera again, stifling another animal cry.

'He'll be all right,' the first man said.

'Just keep him confined to that corner,' said the other man.

Blake heard Greencoats moving, and the clink of metal batons. Ridley was being pushed further back.

'Come on, let's get on with it. Turn her over. I need to get to her lower back.'

'You'll just feel a sharp scratch,' a woman's softer, slightly more saddened words came to Blake now.

One of the men snapped at her: 'Don't talk to them like that. They're not proper people. They don't understand you.'

The cold room went silent. Blake was sweating in the heat glowing from Ridley's body through his glossy hair.

He heard Chimera let out another sigh.

Ridley grunted as Chimera cried out briefly. Blake held onto his fur, as if to tug Ridley back. He'd never be able to hold onto him for a fraction of a second, but he had to try to remind Ridley that he was there and that he needed to remain hidden from the Greencoat keepers.

'There she goes,' the woman's voice said. 'She's out. Shall we extract from her spinal cord first, or from her bone marrow?'

Thirty-Seven

The whole place was silent. Chimera slept on and on. Blake was shaking, standing over her, fighting to contain his anger. Ridley stood next to Blake with worry and care for Chimera written on his face, apparent in the very-near fully human emotions Blake easily discerned playing there.

'How long will she be unconscious?' Blake asked quietly, his face pale, fists clenched. But still he spoke in whispers, as if afraid of waking Chimera. 'How long will she sleep?'

But a single glance from Ridley showed that he did not know. Maybe he couldn't understand Blake's exact words, but their meaning was clear to him.

Outside Chimera's little hut of a house, the lowing cow sang her song. Blake stood over Chimera, listening. It was the saddest and the loveliest thing he had ever heard. He could hear her break down at the end of each breath, starting again, lamenting, stumbling over punctuating sobs.

Then she stopped. Another sound had blundered through, breaking the spell. Another tune sounded out, an electronic noise like a silly imposition from an instrument playing an entirely inappropriate song.

'My phone!' Blake said, only now remembering how it had fallen from his grasp as he scrambled onto the roof away from the Head Hounds.

He moved quickly to the door. Ridley was by his side. Blake looked to see if the big orang-utan was going to stop him from going out. Ridley's face showed him that he was not. They went together, with Ridley covering Blake's body from the view of the closed circuit cameras clustered on top of their mast. Side by side they ran down the road.

Blake felt the assurance of Ridley's protection next to him, his perfumed heat and comfort close by. He felt grateful to the orangutan as he picked his urgent phone from the ground and pressed the button.

His home number was displayed on the screen of the phone, blinking on and off like an angry alarm.

'Where are you?' The voice blared into Blake's ear. 'You'd better tell me where you are and what you're doing!'

Blake breathed, steadying himself. 'Dad, I'm all right,' he said, keeping into the side of the little sloping-roofed house.

'I told you, you weren't to go out!'

From where he crouched, ducking behind the wall-like defence of Ridley's body, he could just see in the distance a man in a green coat tossing slabs of meat to the Head Hounds. 'I know, Dad,' he said, watching the three heads of one hound tearing meat from bones between them.

'Blake, where are you?'

'I'm safe, Dad,' he said. 'Don't worry about me.'

'Don't worry about you! No more of this, Blake, do you hear me?'

'Yes, Dad, I hear.'

'You get home. Now! Right now!'

'OK, Dad,' he said, pushing the button to end the call.

He looked at the camera phone in his hands as he switched it to silent. 'OK, Dad,' he said again. 'I'll be home soon.'

Blake peered round Ridley's body again. He pointed his camera down the street and turned it on to video record. 'I'll be home, as soon as I've finished here,' he said, watching the image being captured, the Greencoats flinging sides of pork, the Head Hounds fighting to tear and to devour, wolfing down the dead flesh, snapping at the breaking bones and swallowing them, too.

Thirty-Eight

Chimera still lay unconscious on her bed, a thin mattress that had been rolled up in one of the corners of the hut. As she breathed deeply, with her perfect face at rest, the creature inhabitants of Innerworld entered nervously.

The Boons filed by without a single grin between them. A stream of tiny Spider monkeys came next, creeping in through the creaking door, leaving their carving knives outside, piling their latest works all round the sleeping mermaid. Two or three gave up a little figurine to Blake as he filmed them. He captured every image. Their little statuettes of cows and mer-girls and orang-utans were focused on film.

Blake had to resist recording every last detail, afraid that his camera memory would not last. He had enough pictures, but wanted to get the disgusted-looking dogs clomping through on two legs with their guinea-pigs and their rabbits scuttling round their hind-paw feet, and the cow, crying at the window.

Then the two white-eyed chimpanzees were there, pictured at the door, arm in arm, peering in. They were the shyest, the gentlest of the primates here. Together they entered the hut, glancing up at Blake behind his phone, gazing down at Chimera.

One spoke to the other. Blake was in no doubt that the series of small grunts and lip-puffs they made towards each other were words.

Outside the hut, lingering in fear, were some of the thinnest pigs alive. They were cruelly emaciated, with ribs on show and sharp, worried features on their fearful faces. These creatures had obviously not supplied the sides of fat pork on which the Head Hounds had been feasting.

But Blake filmed them all as they filed through and went out again, capturing images until the tepid winter sun was too low to allow sufficient light through. Chimera slept on into the afternoon. He captured the tenderness of Ridley, as the giant orang-utan worried over the seal-maiden, as he touched her cheek with a gentle finger.

'I do wish you could talk with me,' Blake whispered to him. 'Chimera – she's like a seal, but she's a person. And you're not just an orang-utan. The cow, the Boons and the Spiders – nothing's just what it appears to be at first.'

Ridley tried to speak to him. He made signs with his colossal hands, attempted to mouth words, held up Chimera's dictionary and shook his head regretfully.

Tucking his phone into his jacket pocket, Blake picked up and held one of Chimera's hands. She began to stir.

Only Blake and Ridley were there with her then, at that moment, with the cow nodding tearfully in the window, as Chimera opened her eyes briefly.

Blake spoke softly, close to her tiny ear. 'Wake up now,' he whispered.

He felt Ridley's hand resting on his shoulder as Chimera's eyes lost contact with consciousness again, as her eyelids closed with a sweep through the air that was almost audible.

Ridley's hand gripped Blake's shoulder gently, giving him a giant's reassurance. Blake placed his hand over Ridley's for a few moments.

Blake stood and looked into Ridley's face as he crouched before him. They were eye to eye. So much passed from one face to the other, from primate to human and back again, that there was practically no difference between them. In that moment, in the contact of their eyes, Blake thought that these complex creatures had tried to communicate very often in the past, that just about every animal alive had had something to say to him, but he'd been too arrogant and too stupid to just stop and look and listen.

'Oh,' Chimera let out a long, aspirated sigh.

Both Blake and Ridley turned to her.

'Chimera!' Blake said. Beside him, he could hear the dusty friction of Ridley's dry palms as he finger-signed his message.

'Both of you,' she smiled. 'Both of you, here, for me.' She made a sign for Ridley.

'How do you feel?' Blake said, sitting by her. 'Are you all right now?'

'I'm strong,' she said. 'I've still got lots of blood left. I'm full to the brim with it.'

Blake smiled now. Ridley tried to, too. 'But why do the Greencoats, why do the labs want to take samples out of your spine and from inside your bones?'

'It's what happens,' said Chimera simply. 'They bring our food. We eat it without asking why.'

'Have you ever asked them why?' Blake said. He'd been listening hard, hiding behind Ridley. 'You never said anything,' he said, 'when they were going to put a needle into your back. You still keep yourself secret. Why not speak to them?'

But Chimera was as silent as she had been with the Greencoats.

'Are you so afraid?' Blake asked, seeing the fear resurfacing in her pained face. 'Are you so afraid of what they'll do to you if they knew you could talk?'

He stopped, waiting for Chimera to answer.

'I have a dream,' she said eventually. 'I told you I dream of a place where I can ... where it's OK for me to speak, where I can move easily, where I'm not always too hot and too heavy.'

'And where is this place?'

She glanced again and again towards Ridley, looking as if she were about to tell him something ... but that was when the screaming started.

Thirty-Nine

From the roof, the tribe cried out.

Ridley shot up, swinging over to the door.

'The Boons again!' Blake said.

'No!' said Chimera, raising herself from the floor. She swayed dizzily. 'No. Not just Boons. Listen.'

As the door crashed wide and Ridley loped out, more primate screams ripped the air of the fading afternoon. Two voices were heard above all the others.

'It's the bonobo – Bonnie and Bonno – help me, Blake, help me to the door.'

Chimera had said she was strong, because she was still full of blood. But the Greencoat scientists had taken so much out of the very marrow of her bones, she had been greatly weakened. She leaned heavily on Blake's shoulders.

'Take it easy,' he was saying. He put his arm around her waist. She was as slim and supple as a sapling tree where her human-like body turned to seal. Blake felt her firm muscles moving warmly under the initial coolness of her skin. 'Don't try and go out,' he said. 'Let me find out what's going on.'

Blake took a look outside. The bonobo chimpanzees were screaming in terror. The Boons on the roof and those still on the ground were stamping, jumping up and down with their mouths wide open, exposing many teeth. The little Spider tribe were scattering, regrouping, scattering again. The tall dogs had picked up their guinea-pig pets protectively and the cow was nowhere to be seen.

Along the darkening lane, a skinny pig was racing in panic, its ever fibrous muscle worn as if just barely under the surface of its skin. Just behind it, an armed gang of Greencoats bristled, fanning out, shifting the little Spiders away with a wave, moving in precise formation, signalling to one another.

Blake felt Chimera very close to him behind the door. They looked out together as the group of Greencoats were homing in on a corner where one house was built against the side of another.

'Don't go out there, Blake,' Chimera said. 'They'll see you. The Greencoats!'

'Why are they doing that?' Blake could see that they had purposely segregated the two bonobo chimpanzees and were trying to separate them.

'They're taking Bonnie!' Chimera exclaimed. 'Oh no! Not Bonnie!'

One of the Green lab people had approached the two terrified chimps with a huge net on a pole. Others amongst them had just poles, sticks to guide or threaten the other villagers to stay out of the way. A few bore arms, rifles, at the ready. The net came down over Bonnie.

'Oh no!' Chimera cried. 'Oh, please, no! Not that!'

'What?' Blake had to ask. 'What is it? What are they doing with her?'

Bonobo Bonnie was being dragged away from her mate, her partner Bonno. He, distraught, was being guided away very roughly by the metal sticks. He screamed at them.

She cried back. Her arms were reaching out through the mesh.

Bonno caught her hand. The sticks were coming down ever harder onto his arms and shoulders. But he held on.

Bonnie was writhing to get out, to get back to Bonno. The net was dragging her further away.

'Why?' asked Blake again.

'They came for her blood a little while ago. Now she's being sent off to Dod.'

'Dod? What's that?'

Chimera said something that Blake could not catch. Bonnie's screams were too loud, Bonno's replies too desperate, combining with the shrieks from the Boons and the shrill squeaks from the Spiders.

Blake could see that Bonno was never going to let her go. He held onto her clutching hand as onto life itself.

Then a rifle was raised against him.

Now a giant roar sounded out, so loud the Head Hounds chained around the village started up with their long, loud howls. But the rifle cracked and Bonno fell as the origin of the great roar ranged into view.

'Ridley!' Chimera cried, as the orang-utan raged towards where Bonno was falling away, hit in the chest, scrabbling across the ground to get back to Bonnie as they dragged her away screaming for him.

'Don't!' Chimera called out.

But another rifle flashed and then another. Ridley reached to his arm and his shoulder.

Blake watched him brushing something out of his fur. 'They couldn't shoot him,' he said, showing too much of himself round the door. 'He's still up! Go, Ridley!'

'Blake!' Chimera dragged him back. 'Don't let them see you. Don't let them find out anything about you.'

Ridley was staggering, bemused, as Chimera held Blake back. Blake felt the strength of her hands on his arm and chest, but he struggled against her until he could see round the door again. Blake just had to see Ridley as he swayed, as he reached out and picked up the limp body of Bonno.

The little chimpanzee flopped in his arms as Ridley staggered as if under a great weight towards Chimera's house. The Greencoats were disappearing with Bonnie towards the entrance to the long corridor into the research centre, while Ridley fell through the door and sat panting and greatly weakened, cradling the Bonobo body in his long, twitching arms.

Forty

Blake couldn't take his eyes from the apparently lifeless Bonno.

Chimera reached out, touching Blake's hand. 'He's unconscious,' she said. 'They've tranquillised him. They hit Ridley too, twice, but it still wasn't enough to put him out.'

Blake looked into the orang-utan's dazed face.

'They'll be back soon,' Chimera was saying. 'They'll tranquillise us all if they think it's necessary, before they let loose the Head Hounds. You must hide.'

Blake's eyes wandered from Ridley to the darkening square of the window, before meeting Chimera's soft stare. He was thinking of his father's voice over the phone, ordering him home.

'You're going,' she said, responding to the look on Blake's face. 'You're going to leave us.'

He didn't say anything. Ridley let a long, gentle grunt of disapproval.

'You can just go away,' Chimera was saying, as the door crept open and the villagers started shuffling in. 'You can just leave this place, because you've got all that – the Outerworld – to go to. And now *we* know, don't we?'

'What do you know?' Blake asked.

'The world – out there – it's not just full of Greencoats. It has people like you in it, and other people too, like you said – people like Ridley, and people like you. It has lots of cows. That place I dream of, Blake, that place I can feel inside me – that's where it is. It has to be out there.'

Blake was looking around at the gathering villagers as they gazed at Chimera. He gazed upon the Spiders and the now-silent Boons, he listened to the lowing cry of the cow. 'The Outerworld,' Blake's head was shaking, 'it's not like – it's more ... '

He looked again at the placidity of the frightened groups congregated in the little hut. 'The Outerworld's more vicious than you'd think,' he said.

'With lions?' Chimera said.

'Yes, lions.'

'And snakes and goats? It was like that, where I used to be. They called us all Chimera, then. That was before they heard the Boons repeating their words. Now they don't say anything, unless they have to. You've heard them, they think we're not proper people.'

'Then you should show them,' Blake said.

Chimera shook her head. 'They'll send me away, away from Ridley, to Dod.'

'Dod?' said Blake. 'You mentioned Dod before – what happens there?'

All round Ridley, as he cradled the too-soundly sleeping Bonno in his red fur, the tiny Spiders collected, punctuated by silent Boons. Just outside the ajar door, the cow's plaintive song started.

'We don't know what happens at Dod,' Chimera said. 'The lions, the snakes and the goats all went there. Lots of others, too. Bonnie, she's gone. Lots go, but nobody ever comes back.'

The cow cried. The door crept further open as the disdainful dogs led in their pets, the rabbits and the guinea-pigs. From outside, a row of skinny pigs blinked and sniffed, creeping ever closer.

'I've heard them talk about it. I've listened to what the Greencoats have said for a long time. They say we help them, help the Greencoats make weapons. Weapons of war.'

Blake stalled for a few moments. He glanced round the various faces looking back at him. He scanned the tiny spider-monkey features, the long-faced Boons, the cats and dogs, the cow, the pigs. The heavy-eyed orang-utan holding onto his unconscious bonobo.

His gaze finished back at the wide-eyed dark and beautiful features of the seal-girl. 'What kind of war?'

96

But Chimera's face told him she was never going to be able to answer his question.

'And where is it, this Dod?'

'It's a secret place,' she whispered just over the sound of the cow's crying song. 'I've heard them say it's *top secret*. But that's where they're sending Bonnie,' Chimera said. 'They took her blood first, now they're sending her there.'

'They took her blood first?' Blake said. 'But doesn't that mean they'll be sending you next?'

She shuddered. 'I don't know. Yes – maybe. I think we'll all have to go there, one day. I don't want,' she said, looking down, blinking slowly, 'I don't want to go there on my own.'

In her eyes, Blake watched the many reflections of himself multiplied by a wash of tears.

All rabbits everywhere stamp on the ground in alarm – but these ones now in the hut on their leads did it softly, their padded feet patting the floorboards rhythmically, in time with the cow's lowing melody, taken up in a few moments by the many Spiders and by the Boons.

Ridley hugged Bonno closer to his chest.

'Why do they make weapons there?' Chimera was asking Blake. 'Why do they want to do that in Dod?'

'I – I don't know, Chimera. They make weapons everywhere.'

'Do they?' she said, blinking once, sweeping a curtain of salt water down her cheeks like the wash of the sea she had never seen. 'Is that what the Outerworld does? Is there no place, nowhere else for my dream to be real in?'

Blake could hardly bear to watch the water shining on her skin. But the room was darkening, Chimera's features fading. He glanced once again through the open window, remembering the worry in his father's voice again. 'I have to—'

'Don't say it,' she whispered. 'You don't belong here, I know.'

The song that the cow sang was amplified now, mimicked closely by serious Boons, punctuated artistically by the sculptor Spiders.

Blake tried to speak, but could say nothing, not now, with the cow's song on everyone's lips but his own. Chimera reached out and touched his cheek. She nodded her seawater-wet features for him to go.

All the villagers were watching, looking up into his face as he took his first step away from the seal-girl. He halted to touch the perfumed fur on Ridley's shoulder. The great orang-utan reached for his hand.

Ridley's huge palm was warm and dustily dry. It held onto Blake for just a simple moment. Then it let him go.

As he stepped through the other village creatures, the rhythm of their song in his ears throbbed with their fear and their sadness.

At the door, surrounded by dogs, cow, monkeys, baboons and pigs, Blake turned to look once more at Chimera. She was keeping as quiet with Blake as she had been with the Greencoats.

Ridley made a sign, speaking for them all, saying goodbye. Blake turned away.

A Boon sat in his way, holding out one of the Unseen Green lab coats. Without it, the Head Hounds would have taken him apart. With it, he'd escape successfully, still in one piece.

But the one piece, the thing he was now, was not the Blake he'd been, arriving on his belly across the wet dawn grass. This Blake, the one leaving now, with the Head Hounds scratching in front and the sad song fading behind, was still in bits, despite the Unseen Green. All his thoughts and feelings, all his beliefs, such as they were before today, had been shattered and scrambled. And fitting them back together again, in any way, new or old, was never going to be an easy task.

Forty-One

More tired than he had ever felt, after the long trek back across the moor, along miles of quiet moonlit road to the small-town cab office, Blake felt light-headed and slightly delirious, as if he were about to burst out laughing, or crying. Walking the deserted streets towards home this late at night was almost as strange as entering the village on the moor and seeing Chimera for the first time. He seemed to be looking at everything with different eyes. Before now, Blake had never really noticed what it was like to be a person, a human being in the world, and not, for example, that fox rummaging in the dustbins over there.

As Blake grew nearer, the fox dropped back into the shadow. Blake stopped and watched it slink by keeping close to the clipped hedge of a front garden, a discarded pizza box in its mouth.

The fox kept a wary eye on Blake where he stood over the other side of the road. Blake gazed back at him, exchanging looks as he had with Ridley, wondering what the world looked like through the eyes of a fox, as it blazed red and wild in the bright light of the streetlamps, sloping away close to garden fences, under the cover of the deep dark behind the opposite hedge.

Blake stood alone, looking up at the closed, curtained windows lined up along the street. He felt himself more in tune with the wary mind of the night-time fox. Foxes knew things that people never would – but maybe Blake now understood what so many others of his kind had missed. Going back to the village, he had wanted to prove his own innocence, nothing more. He had not expected to be staring into the eyes of an orang-utan and feeling the intelligence burning there. He could never have anticipated experiencing the pain of separation felt by an estranged chimpanzee. The sadness of the song the villagers had sung together, and the look in Chimera's eyes, would stay with him now, affecting him for ever.

At home, expecting to find his dad, by this late hour, collapsed back into unintended sleep in the armchair, Blake was surprised to discover him sitting hunched at the kitchen table. The whole place smelled of the sickly sweetness of strong alcohol. His dad was staring into a half full, or far more accurately half empty, glass placed squarely in front of him.

As Blake entered, his dad did not look round. He continued to gaze into the glass for a long, long while. Blake, quietly closing the door behind him, stood by the sink, waiting for a response.

His dad's head turned deliberately, aiming its out-of-focus eyes across the small room.

Blake pointed at the drink on the table. 'Dad! I thought you said—'

He stopped speaking as his father's hand came up and was held there in the air between them.

'Don't!' The voice came from behind the hand, fuzzy and slurred.

Blake waited. He watched his dad lower the hand and look at it, as if wondering what it had been doing there. He watched his dad place the hand, and then the other one, on the tabletop. Slowly, with great difficulty, he stood, turning to face Blake, breathing heavily, swaying slightly. His eyes were reddened, his face was puffy.

'Just – don't,' Blake's dad said, looking round the kitchen, as if for more to drink.

Blake walked quickly to the table and took the glass. He hurried back to the sink and poured the stuff away. Dropping the empty glass into the bowl, turning back, Blake saw that his dad was still standing in the same place, blinking slowly.

He placed one hand back on the table to steady himself. 'I did my best,' he said. 'Always – tried so very hard. It was all for you, in the end.'

'In the end, Dad?'

'All finished,' his father slurred. 'All this?' He looked about again. 'What's it for? All for you, it was. You kept me going. Now – now what do I have?'

'Dad,' Blake said, about to go to him.

The hand came up between them again. 'No. I – don't, Blake. Your mum's not here – she didn't want to, but she had to go from us. A long time. And you – what are you doing, staying out all night after – after you stole those – are you going away too?'

'No, Dad,' he said, with his hand going into his coat pocket, 'I'm not. I had to get something – for you.' He tried to turn the phone on. 'I'll show you.'

'Show me? Show me – what can you show me?'

'Dad, look. The Head Hounds – three heads each. You have to help me now. I don't know what to do about all this, about Ridley and the—'

'Ridley?'

'And the girl. The mermaid, Chimera. They're all here. Look. Please look at this.'

But his dad was swaying towards him. 'Just a nightmare!' he shouted.

'No, Dad! That's what I thought, first of all—'

'This!' The drunk man flung out his arms. 'All this! Now what is it? It's all rubbish – all thrown away. EVERYTHING!'

Blake tried to pull back. He moved away, but his dad's flailing arms flew out and a loose hand swiped the phone from him and sent it clattering across the kitchen floor.

Before Blake could make a move to go and retrieve it, his dad had taken hold of him. He held him tight. For a moment, Blake thought that his father intended to hurt him. But of course that was not so.

'After your mum's illness,' he was whispering close, 'I held you in the chair, do you remember?'

'Yes,' said Blake, holding onto his dad, 'when I told you I didn't want them to take me into care.'

'It all came back to me then,' his dad said, almost too quietly to hear. 'Everything I was for. Remember the trip down the river, do you?'

'Dad . . . '

'Now it's all being taken away again.'

'It isn't, Dad. If you'd only let me show you.' And he ran to collect his phone from the floor. Blake looked at the display panel. 'Oh no!' he exclaimed. 'Oh no – it's broken!'

And his dad almost fell, staggering to the door. 'All of it,' he was saying, shuffling into the other room. 'Broken down. Done with. Everything. All,' he said, falling face-first into the cushions of the settee while his son stood watching in the doorway, clutching a smashed and ruined camera phone.

His father had passed out. Blake went to him and touched his back and turned him over to be sure that he could breathe properly.

He sat down on the floor, one hand holding the broken phone, the other still trying to hold on to his one surviving parent. 'What am I supposed to do now, Dad?' he sighed. 'What can I do about anything, with everything broken and without you, without even my best friend to turn to?'

Forty-Two

More than half of Monday morning had gone before he woke fully dressed on his bed. Blake jumped awake, with a line of spit oozing from one side of his mouth.

In his hand, as he sat up, an irreparable mobile phone. He looked at it, before peering about his room. His pretty-girl movie posters did not seem to make any sense. They smiled down at him as ever, but seemed to be expecting a response he was unable to deliver. They did not look real now, in any conceivable way, smiling stupidly like that, from heads full of much too much hair.

Blake looked at the clock on his bedside cabinet. 'Oh, no!'

He got up, surprised to find his trainers still on his feet. Downstairs, there was no sign of his dad. The kitchen was a mess.

Blake did the washing up and then went to take a quick shower. Back in the kitchen, over a big bowl of cereal, Blake sat looking at his broken mobile. He was ridiculously late for school once more. Tonight he was due to register at the police station again.

He hoped his dad had gone to work. Blake could only assume that he had. But the very fact that he had gone out without trying to wake his son for school said a lot. It was saying something that Blake wasn't ready to face yet, something hard to take, about his father submitting, giving up on the son he now believed he had lost . . .

No, Blake was not prepared enough to think all that through. He was ready only for school, however late in the day it was.

Going out of the front door, he met his dad about to come in.

Blake opened the door and there he was, grey-faced, with a big bottle of lemonade and a newspaper in his hands.

Blake stepped through the door and they stood together for a moment. But the moment passed too quickly and his dad was looking down and stepping into the house without a word to his son.

Forty-Three

He stood on his own facing the door. From somewhere not far off, voices in song came to him in snatches. Blake's head was filled immediately with memories of the moorland villagers all gathered to mourn Bonno's loss.

Blake watched his own hand stretching forward and knocking gently on the door.

'Come!'

He inhaled deeply.

Mrs Gordon looked up in surprise as Blake entered her office. Sitting back in her chair behind the desk, she put down her pen and smiled. 'Blake,' she said, standing. 'Come in, come in. I'm very glad to see you.'

'I've only just got here,' Blake admitted, still listening out for snatches of sad songs, still experiencing the sense of loss the villagers felt – that he had felt, with the door closing with such finality between him and his dad. 'I'm late again, sorry.'

'Yes,' she smiled, indicating that he should sit. 'They told me you weren't in this morning.'

'My dad, he was – not very well.'

'Ah. So you had to stay at home and look after him?'

'No. It was just that he didn't wake me up.'

'And you slept in ...'

'I – I was out late last night.' He had to own up, suspecting that the headteacher had much more information on him than she was letting on.

'And where did you go to, out so late last night, Blake? Can you tell me?'

He wanted to explain it all – the village, the villagers, Chimera watching him with her big black eyes as he was leaving her again – but to his dad, not Mrs Gordon.

'Blake?' she was saying, because he had been sitting thinking for too long, lost in the feelings he'd brought away with him. 'Blake?' she said again. 'The Underworld – have you been back there?'

He knew that she did not mean an actual place. He wished she did, but the Underworld was being translated into a delusion, a mirage brought about by what Blake was supposed to have been taking.

'No,' he said emphatically. 'I haven't been to the Underworld.'

Because, he was thinking, the Underworld of ghouls and monsters has never existed. The Innerworld however . . .

'Where were you, then?' she asked. 'Out until late last night?'

He gazed into the pattern of her carpet as he had the Friday before this weekend. Back then he saw terrors writhing. Now, cows crying.

'Blake? Can you answer me?'

'No,' he said softly. There was so much he had yet to find out, to try to understand. 'There's nothing to tell,' he said. 'My dad's unhappy. I had to get out of the house.'

But she was looking too closely, boring into him too deeply to allow him to hold hard enough onto his lies to stare her out. 'I want to get back to my studies,' he said.

She nodded, without breaking her solid gaze. 'That's good. That's very good.'

'I need to pass Biology,' he said. 'I'd like to, if I could, do some studying on my own.'

'On your own?' she said, with raised eyebrows.

'I just need to look up some things. I've been – finding out about – things. Orang-utans. Bonobos.'

'Oh, bonobos.'

'Yes,' he said, looking up in surprise, because her voice had registered recognition. 'Bonobos.'

'I saw a television programme about them,' Mrs Gordon said. 'Chimpanzees.'

'Not *just* chimpanzees,' Blake said.

'No, indeed not. They're smaller, less aggressive and – more caring, aren't they?'

'Yes,' said Blake, trying not to give away too much of what he was feeling.

The head teacher regarded him carefully, for a long, long while. But Blake was unable to return her gaze, remembering Bonnie and Bonno being dragged apart, crying out for each other.

'Yes, indeed,' Mrs Gordon said at long last. 'The bonobo are more caring. Is that what has attracted you to them, in particular, Blake?'

Under her steady stare, Blake understood that Mrs Gordon was thinking of his father. She was picturing Blake casting about for the love he was missing from the damaged relationship with his dad. Her face showed the pity she was feeling.

Blake's face, at the same time, reflected pity. But his feelings were for the bonobo, the love that he had witnessed between them that was real, and was theirs, not his.

Forty-Four

Mrs Gordon took Blake to the computer room. It was full of Business Studies students looking into the design of different web sites. After a quick conversation between the Head and the class tutor, two very curious girls were shifted from their terminal to share with another two and Blake given access to the internet.

'There,' Mrs Gordon said, placing paper pad and pencils by his elbow on the table. 'Is there anything else you need, Blake? Then I'll leave you to it.'

Blake sat staring at the search engine page. In the reflection of the computer screen he could make out the headteacher talking to the other teacher behind him. Then the Business Studies tutor crossed to the other side of the room, leaving Mrs Gordon standing there quietly on her own.

He waited a few more moments for her to move away. When it became clear that she was staying, Blake typed in his first word. Bonobo.

And there they were. Bonobo – smaller chimpanzees, originating from an area in Congo, in Africa. They looked the same, except for the eyes. These ordinary bonobo, unaggressive, more caring, gentler though they were, had ordinary Chimpanzee eyes. Their eyes were brown, not blazing white.

Mrs Gordon leaned in over his shoulder to better see the Bonobo, then to stare at an orang-utan, the next image up. Blake felt her presence behind him, examining the impression of the big red primate. She, he knew, saw an ape, while he saw Ridley signing, communicating intelligently with the other villagers.

Blake showed her baboons screaming, not laughing, spider monkeys without artistic tendencies. He did not bother to go to the dogs on their four legs, or rabbits without rhythm, or cows with no songs to sing. He showed the headteacher a seal that looked nothing like a girl. And had he plugged in the word girl, Blake knew, it would have shown nothing like a seal.

But she was both. How?

Turning to the pad of paper by his side, he jotted down the single word. Her name.

Mrs Gordon still lingered over his shoulder in silhouette as his fingers lingered on the computer keys. He tapped a single C and then stopped. He was being watched.

Again he tapped once.

H I M E R A

Blake stopped. He moved the cursor to 'Find Images'.

He clicked on the button.

Mrs Gordon disappeared, as if devoured by the thing he found that seemed to leap out into Blake's horrified face.

Forty-Five

Mrs Gordon said he should concentrate on the more caring bonobo and forget about the furious fantasies of ancient Greece. Blake tried to assure her that he was all right now; that his reaction to what he saw was just surprise, not fear, or terror.

He had to wait until the Head finally left him there before asking the class teacher if he could print a page to take away with him. A single, simple sheet with a drawing on was folded into his inside pocket. And inside his head now, as on the printed page, a more ancient, far more appalling creature, another Chimera altogether, from a very different legend.

PART TWO

The
Innerworld

Forty-Six

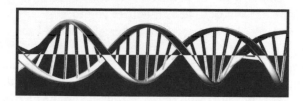

On his way out of school, Blake was lost in thought, attacked by his own imagination, when Alfie appeared.

'All right, Blake?' Alfie said, with some urgency.

The roaring monsters receded from Blake's ears. He looked at Alfie, surprised to see him there. 'Yeah,' he said. 'I'm all right.'

'Knew you would be,' Alfie said. 'Look, mate. Sorry about the other day. I didn't mean to say I thought that of you – with the drugs.'

'Ah,' said Blake. 'Forget it.'

'No,' Alfie insisted. 'No, I can't. I'm sorry about it. Blake, hang on a minute. Wait. Listen – I didn't think it, but others did.'

'Others? What others?'

'Well, you know what my mum's like. She's always going into one over something or other.'

Blake nodded. He had, on several occasions when they were smaller, been quite frightened by the way Alfie's mother would tear into him, for the most trivial of reasons.

'Well, she's – hang on a minute, Blake – listen. She's outside. Waiting. I know she is. And loads of others. Sorry, mate. It's not me. I tried to stop her. She's lost it, totally, after the police came round to our house and told her – everything.'

Blake started to move away. He didn't want to hear what the police had been telling Alfie's mum.

'Look,' Alfie said, 'I'll meet you, yeah? Up the town? Let's go up the mall, like we used to.'

'Can't,' said Blake, about to leave the building. 'I've got to go sign in at the police station. Got to go.'

Alfie had stopped short of the door. 'I'll follow you up,' he called as Blake went out, 'in a while. See you there!'

Blake heard Alfie's voice calling after him behind the closing exit door of the school. And straightaway he could see Alfie's mum red in the face by the school gates, her tight-lipped mouth chewing over angered words. The ranks of her posse had swollen over the weekend, as a result of the headlines and the pictures and stories in the papers. They looked like a lynch mob.

With his legs growing ever heavier under him, Blake's walking speed diminished almost to a halt. He couldn't see how he was going to get through unscathed. There was no other way out of the school grounds. Then he thought of facing the Head Hounds. He remembered them roaring into his face as he pressed his back against the dead-end of the solid village dwellings. What could possibly be more intimidating than that?

Then there was a voice beside him suddenly, telling him not to worry. Blake looked round at Mrs Gordon's reassuring smile. Blake was going to try to show her he needed no reassurance, but she was too busy studying the mood of the mob at the gates.

'Thank you all!' she said, very loudly, walking straight up to Alfie's mother. 'Thank you so much for wanting to demonstrate your concern!' She was looking into all the faces, at the stilled jaws, the shifty, childishly in-trouble-now eyes.

'It shows such a wonderful sense of community,' Mrs Gordon held them with her school-assembly voice and her almost angry demeanour.

'And so many faces I haven't seen for such a long time!' Blake heard her saying as he passed through the crowd. The accused faces looked away and just let him through, eyes cast to the ground like a gang of caught-out kids.

'As much as I appreciate your concern,' Blake heard the Head saying behind him as he made his way up the street, 'discipline and the law will be upheld by appropriate means in my school. If you do wish to be involved, there is a vacancy on the board of school governors that needs to be filled by ... '

Blake glanced round. Only one of the downcast faces came up

to look back at him. As Blake fingered the single sheet inside his jacket, Alfie's mum's face reared up at him. The page was printed with the 'Chimera' of ancient Greek legend – he pictured Alfie's mum goat-stamping the ground as she gritted growling like a spiky lion, spitting something near to serpent venom down her three-faced chin.

Forty-Seven

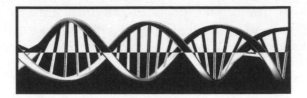

Mrs Gordon, calming the hysterical parents with her best lecturing teacher's voice, waited until Blake was safely out of the way before dismissing them.

The parents were afraid of Blake because he represented for them everything that threatened their children on the streets and in their schools. She did not blame them, and was more than adequately experienced to deal with and to dissipate their mob mentality.

But Blake was altogether far more interesting. The way the boy had reacted to that goat-lion-serpent image on the computer screen showed some kind of deeper, darker disturbance. No, there was far more to this than Blake Newton's drug crime alone. Why would a boy like that, an over-achieving athlete, go so far off the rails in the first place?

As head teacher, Mrs Gordon could not just let this pass. She took her responsibilities far too seriously to ignore Blake's pain and not take action to try to discover the root cause of her pupil's psychological problem.

Forty-Eight

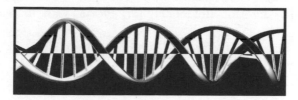

The press hadn't been there on Blake's entry into the building, but they had collected in competitive groups as he came out, calling to him, trying to get him to stop.

As he trammelled up the road with his hand shielding his face from the probe of the long lens cameras, Alfie appeared again, just as before.

'All right, Blake?'

'Blake Newton?' the reporters were calling to them from the other side of the street. 'What about a bit of a smile, just for the cameras?'

'Wow!' Alfie exclaimed, stumping along next to him as Blake almost ran to escape. 'Have a look at that lot!'

'Blake Newton!'

'Blake!' they shouted, clamouring after them.

'Come on!' Blake said to Alfie.

But Alfie had stopped, turning to look, with a broad grin, at the pack of newshounds behind them.

Blake had to grab his friend by the scruff of his neck and drag him away. One of the reporters ran up to Blake and handed him a card. 'Call me,' he hissed. 'There's money in it.'

'Thanks, Alfie!' someone else called out.

Blake dragged him harder. 'What did he say?' he asked. They were running together now, leaving the pack behind. 'What did he call you?' he asked Alfie again, when they were far enough away.

'I don't know,' Alfie said. 'I didn't hear.'

'I did!' Blake said, glancing at the card the reporter had given him. 'He called you Alfie!'

'Yeah?' said Alfie, still looking very pleased with himself. 'Did he?'

'Yes, he did.' Blake grabbed him by the front of his jacket.

'Easy!' Alfie's grin slipped.

'He called you Alfie! He knows your name!'

'Yeah? And?'

'*And?* How does he know? How do they know who you are?'

'I don't know,' Alfie said, shoving Blake's hands away, marching towards the mall. 'You need to calm down, mate!'

Blake stood on his own for a few moments longer, thinking. Tucking the card into his pocket, he turned and watched Alfie stumping up the street. 'Hang on!' he called.

Alfie did not stop.

Blake ran up beside him. 'Alfie. Hold on, slow down. I'm sorry. I suppose they know everything by now. All my friends' names.'

Alfie didn't say anything now. Side by side they walked through the bus station to the shops. Blake was wondering how much to tell Alfie of his experiences – shaking hands with Ridley, laughing with the Boons, singing with a crying cow, gazing into Chimera's eyes. He wondered how to even begin to describe the overwhelming effect it had had on him. And he wondered what effect it would have on Alfie, as he watched him bouncing along in his super-white trainers under his short cropped hair, putting into his pierced lobes the diamond earrings that he wasn't allowed to wear in school.

'Anyway,' Alfie said suddenly, 'what difference would it make?'

'Would what make?'

'Talking to them. Talking to everyone. The police are going to interview us all, everyone on the trip. Did you know that?'

Blake tried to slow their pace to get a better look at his best friend's face. But Alfie was rushing ahead, springing off the balls of his feet as he always did, lunging forward as if in a hurry to get somewhere.

'The police can talk to everybody,' Blake said, 'but the papers can't.'

'What difference does it make?'

'Lots of difference, Alfie! Stuff gets out about me that isn't true!'

'Like what? What isn't true?'

They were entering the shopping mall by this time, passing through the automatic doors. Blake turned, just inside, taking Alfie by the shoulder, stopping him.

'What are you saying? Have you been talking to them?'

'Well, what difference does it make?' Alfie said once again, shrugging off Blake's hand. 'Everyone's going to find out, anyway. I'm still your mate.'

'Are you?'

'Course! I don't care what you took.'

'What? You – what, did they pay you? Did they?'

Alfie couldn't keep the smirk from his face. 'It's me to buy the burgers then, yeah?' he said, swinging away.

Blake stood, dumbfounded. Who was there to trust, here, stuck in the Outerworld where everyone disbelieved everyone else? Why was Alfie here, now? What did he want to find out? And how much did he want to sell his friend for?

Alfie had reminded Blake not to forget who his friends were. And Blake had thought, instantly, of an orang-utan and a mermaid.

Forty-Nine

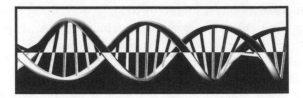

'Look who's outside the burger bar again!' Alfie was grinning as Blake caught up with him.

Blake was just about to take Alfie by the front of his jacket. But Alfie was moving away fast, pointing and smirking at the people demonstrating in the middle of the shopping centre with their placards and their little leaflets.

'Oi!' Alfie was calling out. He turned back to Blake. 'See? Veggie Vanessa and her street crew!' He turned away. 'Oi! Meat is murder!'

Blake had halted on the spot as Vanessa's head twitched in his direction. She stood there, leaning to one side as she had to, to maintain her balance. She was looking past Alfie to Blake.

'Meat is murder!' Alfie was blaring out. 'Yeah, and I could murder a decent burger!' He laughed.

Alfie was practically laughing in Vanessa's face. Her mother was not there, as far as Blake could see, only some of her anti-vivisectionist friends from school.

'Have a leaflet,' Vanessa was saying, determined not to be intimidated by Alfie, even with his grinning mug shoved into her personal space.

'Yeah,' Alfie glanced back at his best mate, 'I'll have one. Thanks,' he said, taking it from Vanessa. He took a bite out of it, tearing off the corner with his teeth.

A couple of girls Alfie and Blake knew had stopped to watch.

Alfie bit another corner. About half the sheet of paper was being chewed up in his mouth. 'Mmmm!' he was nodding, looking about, showing off to the cool girls with their shopping bags, watching out for Blake as he approached.

Then Alfie's face changed. He put on a serious, disgusted guise, as if he'd suddenly got a taste of what he was eating. 'Pah!' he gagged, spitting out the papier-mâché blob onto the hard tiled floor at Vanessa's feet. 'It's veg!' he roared into her face.

Vanessa was white, her head twitching to one side. She was trying to say something, but it would not come out.

'That's what you veggies eat, that is!' Alfie shouted at her. 'You stinking carrot-munchers. Eat this!' he yelled.

It looked as if he were about to try to shove what was left of the pamphlet into Vanessa's mouth. He never got that far. His arm was yanked back, spinning him round. Then Blake had him by the front of his jacket, almost lifting him off his feet.

'Get off me!' Alfie shoved him away. 'They're right about you,' he said.

Blake stormed up to him. 'What would you know? What would anybody know? She's got it right!' he said, glancing at Vanessa as she gazed at them, frightened. 'She makes you look like an idiot!' he raged at Alfie.

Alfie, shocked at the strength of his friend's attack, fell back. 'You're the idiot,' he said, without conviction.

'Oh, yeah?' Blake took another look at Vanessa. He went to put a hand out to her, before changing his mind. 'What would we do,' he said, as if to Vanessa, 'if cows could cry?' He looked back at Alfie. 'What would we do if they sang sad songs? Make burgers out of them? Would we?'

'You've lost it, mate,' Alfie said, all the time stepping away. 'You've lost it big time.'

'Have I?' said Blake, stepping after him. 'Well, maybe I have. Because nothing's like you think it is, Alfie! People like you – you and your mad mum and all her followers back there – none of you have got a clue.'

'And you have, I suppose, have you?' Alfie said. 'You and people like her, like meat-is-murder there – you know it all, do you?'

'No, I don't. Not all of it. But I do know that Vanessa's one of the bravest people in the world, and she's right. And one day, she's going to win.'

Fifty

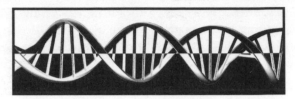

'Are you all right?' Vanessa was by his side, looking up at him timidly.

Blake was staring down the avenue between the shops at Alfie as he made quickly away, turning every now and then to make a sign at Blake. Alfie pretended to turn a loose screw in the side of his head, before pointing at Blake.

'Blake?' Vanessa said softly.

Then his head was spinning. The Outerworld whirled round and round him in a confusion of synthetic environments – streets and shopping centres and motorways swept him up and threatened to bowl him over.

'Are you OK?' Vanessa's gentle voice entered Blake's subconscious as if from the ground, anchoring the turn and teem of the dizzying opulence of the shops and bustling shoppers. Everything tumbled into the centre of concentration that was now Vanessa's face in Blake's.

He steadied himself by staring back at her. From the corner of his eye, he could see the girls from school still there behind their armour of shopping bags, wondering what to make of him. Blake took some leaflets from Vanessa and turned to the girls. 'If you want to find something out,' he said.

They moved away from him without taking an information sheet. Blake was left gazing through the window of the burger bar.

'Come with me,' Vanessa said, touching his arm, leading him

away from the sight of so many jaws moving at once. 'Come over here and sit down.'

Blake let her draw him to a vacant seat by the side of the potted plastic plants. He kicked away an empty drinks bottle and a take-away carton before sitting down next to her.

'Do you know what the word anthropomorphism means?' she said.

He didn't say anything. There was just too much going on in his head.

'It means giving animals human tendencies. It's what we do to our pets. We look at them as if they were like us. But they're not. They're as they are, or at least they should be, if we didn't breed changes into them, giving them characteristics to please only ourselves.'

'But what if they were?' Blake asked. 'What if they were and we weren't any different from them? What if we were all one of the same thing?'

'We are!' Vanessa said, smiling broadly. 'Evolution has separated us. We were the lucky ones. We ended up with the greatest power – intelligence! But go back far enough, we're all from common ancestry – us, all mammals, birds, reptiles, fish – even trees. We *are* all the one single thing, Blake, that's what we've forgotten.'

'But – but . . . ' Blake was stammering after what he wanted to say. 'But what if – what if something happened – to make us join up again? What if a person and an animal – an animal with a person's—'

'A chimera, you mean?' Vanessa said, devastating Blake with the ease with which she just came out with that very special name.

'Chimera?' he gasped.

Vanessa's twitching had stopped. She watched Blake steadily as he reached into his inside pocket, bringing out and unfolding the piece of paper.

'Chimera!' he said, handing her the opened sheet.

'Yes,' she said, looking at the monstrous image. 'That's where the word comes from. It was this thing in the Greek – I *think* Greek – fables. But now chimera has come to mean any kind of

123

transgenic, I mean cross-species creature – especially a combination of human and something else.'

'Like – like a human being and a seal?'

'Yes, I suppose—'

But Blake had jumped up from the seat on which they sat together. 'A person and a seal – that would be a chimera?'

'Yes,' Vanessa reached out to him. 'What's wrong?'

'Wait a minute!' Blake was turning in circles. 'Hang on, hang on.'

'Blake—' Vanessa was struggling to get up from the seat, concentrating on his animated, excited face.

'I can't think,' Blake was shaking. 'Chimera,' he said, feeling the word in his mouth again, as if trying out its various meanings. 'Chimera. She said they were all called that, once.'

Vanessa placed a calming hand on his arm. 'Blake,' she said again, glancing left and right, 'you really need to calm down.'

He was staring into her face, as if looking there for more meanings to the one word. 'They're *all* chimeras,' he whispered, as if to himself.

Blake stood, breathing, breathing. The single word, the name and its other definitions were coming at him from every direction.

'We're almost finished here,' Vanessa was saying, glancing towards her friends. 'Stay there, Blake. Let me get my things.'

He watched her as she walked to where the others with her were still trying to give out leaflets. He wanted to say something, to try to put words to how he was feeling, but only one would come to him. He whispered it again: 'Chimera. Chimera.'

Vanessa returned lugging her bags of many leaflets and booklets in a hefty carrier, with a shoulder bag slung across her angled body.

'Let me take that,' Blake said, relieving her of the carrier. He enjoyed the weight of it in his hand. His muscle reflexes were firing. He wanted to run, to sprint, to use up some of the energy of excitement coursing through his veins.

In a coffee house at one end of the mall, Vanessa chose a table tucked away from everyone else. She settled herself with her bags as Blake spilled the tea he carried over. He clumped the cups too heavily onto the table-top, clambering across into a seat in the corner, drumming his fingers, tapping his toes.

Vanessa took a sip of her hot tea, peering at him over the edge of her steamy cup while he piled sugar into his own. 'Tell me, Blake,' she said, in not much more than an elevated whisper, 'tell me what's so disturbing to you about that picture, the Chimera?'

He looked at her for a long time. His juddering legs went still, his half-fisted hands left lying on the table left and right of his teacup and saucer. 'I've seen them,' he said, leaning forward to whisper close to Vanessa's ear.

She drew back. 'You've seen chimeras?'

He nodded, severely.

'But,' she said, choosing her words carefully, 'but we've all seen them.'

Blake drew away now.

'All of us on that trip,' Vanessa went on. 'We all saw a chimera.'

Fifty-One

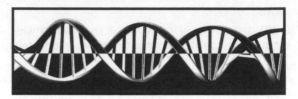

'Chimera?' Blake was gasping in astonishment. 'You saw her?'

'Her?' Vanessa squinted up at him. 'Could be. But we all saw her, everyone from the coach. The mouse.'

'The Supermouse?'

'No, no. The other mouse, the one in which they'd genetically engineered to have cells more like human ones. The one they were going to give polio to. That was a chimera. Its DNA had been altered, combined with human DNA in a particular way.'

'How do you know all this?'

'I study it. I don't agree with it, but I do study it. I want to devote my life to understanding and objecting to the bad things that are being done for my sake, supposedly in my name. I know they can chop out a tiny piece of the mouse DNA and put in a bit of human DNA. It gives the mouse cells the information how to build.'

'And they can do this – in the research labs?'

'Oh, yes. And lots more. All over the world these things are being done. To do that to that mouse was quite easy – relatively. They can't always tell what the combinations of different DNA are going to give. Did you know that someone somewhere has made rabbits that glow in the dark by combining their DNA with that of a jellyfish? All these things, the mice with altered cells, glowing rabbits, totally transparent fish, all sorts of things are being done – here, let me show you.'

Blake watched her delve into her shoulder bag, bringing out a very slim silver notebook computer.

'I think I can go online in here,' she said, flipping the lid, turning on the computer.

Blake moved round the table to sit next to Vanessa as she worked through the network connections. 'Glowing rabbits?' he said.

So Vanessa tapped out those two words on her keyboard and pressed the enter button. She began to read out loud:

'"Turn a special light on the fluffy white rabbit called Alba and she glows light green, a feat of genetic engineering that's sparked a storm of controversy among medical ethicists and animal rights campaigners. Alba was born with that quality because, as an embryo, she was injected with DNA from a phosphorescent jellyfish. And she is now isolated in a French laboratory because of protests and questions about what would happen if she reproduces."

See what they can do – what is being done? – look, look at these.' She was pointing at the screen.

Blake peered in.

'Transgenic pigs,' Vanessa was saying, 'with both mouse and bacterial chromosomes. A Rhesus monkey with jellyfish genes – jellyfish again! Transgenic mice – we've already seen those.'

'But these are all just animals – I mean animals with just ... other animals. No humans, no human genes.'

'Yes, because creating transgenic chimeras with humans has been disallowed pretty well everywhere in the world, until ... '

'Until?' Blake was watching Vanessa pressing the buttons again. His attention turned back to the screen, to the title of the article Vanessa's search engine had brought up.

'About Hybrids and Chimeras.'

'"Britain Approves Use of Hybrid Human-Animal Embryos,"' Vanessa was reading to him. '"British plans to allow scientists to use hybrid animal–human embryos for research has won final approval from British lawmakers."'

Blake looked at her again. 'They're allowed to do it?' he gasped. 'They're allowed to make cross-breeds between people and animals?'

'So far, only in Britain,' Vanessa said. 'Scientists say the embryos would not be allowed to develop for more than fourteen days. They're supposed to be able to harvest stem cells – the cells that haven't yet decided what type of tissue they're going to turn into. But listen ... listen to this: "British researchers say they have created embryos and stem cells using human cells and the egg cells of cows, but said such experiments would not lead to hybrid human–animal babies, or even to direct medical therapies."'

Blake was trying to keep up with Vanessa. He was struggling with all the information coming at him.

'Did you get that, Blake?' she was saying. 'Such experiments would not lead to hybrid human–animal babies, or even to direct medical therapies. If they won't lead to medical therapies, what's the point in doing them?'

'To see if they can?' Blake said.

'Yes – yes! And, do you believe it, that these human-based animal embryos won't eventually lead to hybrid babies? Do you believe that all the embryos will be destroyed after a couple of weeks, and that nobody's ever, ever going to try to grow these things into—'

'Into chimeras,' Blake said.

Fifty-Two

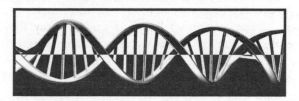

'Into chimeras,' Vanessa repeated. 'It's going to happen, Blake, one day.'

'It *is* happening,' he said, looking all round to see if anyone was watching or listening to them. But they were alone. 'I *know* it's happening.'

'Yes,' Vanessa said, getting quite as excited as Blake now. 'I'm sure of it too. Someone, somewhere is doing it.'

'I've seen them,' Blake hissed. 'The Greencoats, those scientists doing experiments on them, taking samples from the spine and right out of the middle of the bones.'

'Then something should be done about it,' Vanessa said. 'This type of research should be public. If it's happening, someone needs to show everyone what's going on.'

'That was what this was supposed to do,' said Blake, slamming down the broken mobile phone from his pocket. 'It was all there, ready to show the world.'

'What is it?' Vanessa said, looking at the smashed screen and the broken buttons. 'What's on there?'

'Chimera,' Blake said. 'Ridley, Chimera, the Boons, the Spiders, the cow.' He was shaking. 'Listen – they're doing experiments. Weapons experiments. That's why they send them away to Dod.'

'Dod?'

'Do you know it? They take blood to test their stem cells and then they send them there!'

'Oh, the D.O.D.,' Vanessa then said. 'The Department of Defence – is that what you mean?'

'Yes!' Blake understood immediately. He was yelling, almost jumping out of his seat.

'Keep your voice down.' She ducked, hissing at him.

'Now I see it – the Department of Defence – the Ministry of Defence – weapons of war – the Head Hounds!'

Vanessa was still trying to quieten him.

'Where did *they* come from?' he went on. 'Defence, attack. Do you think the army would be interested in the Head Hounds, in massive ferocious Cerberus dogs with three heads you can train to do what you want? Do you think they'd be interested in something like this?' he said, unfolding his black and white picture of the goat-headed, lion-headed, serpent-tailed terror of the ancient myths of Greece.

But Vanessa had turned back to her screen, tapping in the letters DOD. 'Look,' she was saying, staring in horror.

'"Defence Department Sponsors Aggressive Stem Cell Research."'

'Blake,' Vanessa was saying, trying to control the twitching of her nervous muscles. 'Tell me what you've seen. Please. Tell me all of it.'

'They took blood from her spine. They wanted the stem cells.'

'Took from whom?'

'No!' he said, crunching the piece of paper into a ball in his fist. 'No, they won't send her there. I won't let them.'

Vanessa reached out to him. 'Don't go! What will you do? Blake. *Blake!*'

But he was already striding away from her.

'Let me help you!' she cried out.

'You have,' he called back as he left the cafe. 'You already have.'

Vanessa went to call out for Blake again. She would have gone after him, but he was too fast, much too fast for her, like the athlete he still was.

All Vanessa could do was stalk to the door to watch the runner sprinting away at what appeared to be Olympic speed, before looking back at the broken mobile phone he had left next to her notebook computer on the tea-stained table.

Fifty-Three

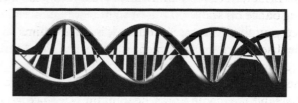

Blake wasn't worried about having left such a message as he came out of the phone booth, tucking the reporter's card back into his pocket. He knew that once the reporter received this, he'd be there: 'Hi, this is Blake Newton,' he had spoken very carefully into the public telephone mouthpiece. 'I've got the real story about the drugs I was supposed to have stolen from the research centre. I'm going there now. There's something you need to understand about that place. Meet me on the street right outside the research centre car park tomorrow morning, seven a.m., and I'll tell you – I'll show you.'

What was really troubling Blake, at this moment, was the number of clouds rolling across the sky in front of the moon. Mid-winter, and it was dark not long after school finished. Withdrawing the last of his savings from the cash machine outside the bank, he noticed the streetlamps were already coming on, the headlights from the cars shining across the surface of the road. Over the rooftops to the west, the sky was reflecting red onto those clouds clinging to the horizon. A road-gritting lorry passed too close to the kerb near Blake as he counted his money, clinking brown sandy salt all over his shoes.

Then he had to wait until well after night fell, sitting in the taxi-rank until the driver arrived. On his way at last, the high, small moon followed Blake in the side window of the car. It kept disappearing behind the broken clouds, coming out again and appearing to run alongside the cab.

'Here?' the confused cabbie asked Blake, dropping him off on the dark, moonlit road across the freezing moor.

Blake thanked and paid him without answering his question. He watched the car move off out of sight before undertaking the trudge across the open moorland to where he was certain, this time, he had hidden the Unseen Green lab coat.

Every time the clouds closed in across the high bright moon, Blake stumbled over the wet-sponge surface with practically no visibility at all. Even with the moon out, the low shadows cast by the dense, uneven grasses tripped him at every other step. Time after time he was sent sprawling, bouncing and turning in the wet and the near-freezing cold.

But it was not just the hard work of walking that warmed him. It was as if Blake were carrying extra weight now, loaded down by his new knowledge. Nobody outside the scientific organisations knew what was going on here. And then nobody but Blake in the whole of the Outerworld knew what Chimera and Ridley were really like. It was not just experiments on defenceless animals Blake was fighting against, but the abuse of thinking, emotional beings. Exposing the abuse, showing the world the truth, was the only way he was ever going to save Chimera from Dod, and all the horror he was certain happened there. He had to do this, to get the newspapers to show just what cruelty was being committed in the name of defence ... which was all about war.

The fear he had seen in Chimera's face, the confusion in Ridley's as he'd hugged the tranquillised body of Bonno, was never far from Blake's consciousness as he bounced across the grass looking for the conspicuous stone under which he had hidden the Unseen Green. There it was, exactly as he remembered it from yesterday, but glistening now under a layer of frost. He wrapped himself tightly in green and stood outside the sheep-pen ring round the village, gazing up at the sky.

The clouds had all but cleared, leaving a starry sky that seemed to be scattering frosty sparks on the ground. The vicious sheep were there, tearing up and crunching frozen grass. They themselves, from this distance, looked like the small clouds dropped to clear the way for moon and starlight.

One or two horned heads turned as Blake passed through the

sheep-field periphery of the village. He stumbled on, with thistles tangled in his laces, hard stems scratching under the bottoms of his trouser legs.

Under the next fence and down the hill into the valley and Blake entered the silent village. In its centre, he could make out the red indicator lights of the cameras blinking on and off on their high stem. He passed through the little wood and turned away from the street that was policed by the CCTV. Running quickly round the backs of the houses, Blake heard the first of the sounds.

Sniffing. Many noses, snuffling against the ground.

Blake heard them before he saw the first Hound. It rounded the corner, one, two, three heads appearing. All noses to the aromatic ground, the beast had its mauve-black hackles up, its broad and bony shoulders hunched, with every muscle primed. Three more heads appeared. They sniffed, they took turns in looking.

Frozen to the icy ground, Blake wrapped himself closer in Unseen Green. He stood like a Spider-carved statue while the pack of Head Hounds gathered about him. His scent must have wafted everywhere. From all directions they homed in on it, endlessly snuffling it up, looking out, sniffing and looking in shifts, three heads working for once in unison.

It was impossible to count them. So many were gathered together now, it looked like a sea of heads. But so many snouts must have sucked up every interesting scent, as they started to sit, to lick themselves, with one or two mouths endlessly growling at two or three others.

Blake stood for what felt like an age until he was sure that they were not aware of him. He tried a tentative step between two huge black bodies. They took no notice. He tiptoed between them, keeping a careful watch for the tails lying on the ground – it was like stepping between dark islands in an ocean of moonlight.

Accidentally kicking one Hound's foot, its three heads swung towards him in horrifying simultaneity. The heads' six eyes glinted palely. As one, their lips came up and the triple-growl rumbled at Blake where he stood petrified. But one by one the three heads lost interest and turned away.

Blake was able to breathe again. He stepped, carefully, carefully, towards the door of Chimera's little house, until he could just make out the grain of the wood. Even in the pale white moonlight, the Unseen Green had done its job. He was nearly there.

So very close – and then the moon went in, behind a lonely little cloud.

Fifty-Four

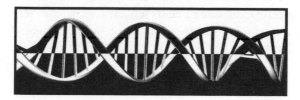

The village was plunged into the dark of moonless mid-winter night. Now that the green was truly unseen, there was only scent left to go by. The Hounds' senses were heightened, their multi-heads snapping to attention.

Blake dashed the last small distance to the door. His hand touched the wood, when what sounded like a thousand howls ripped through the air. As if the noise had hold of him, Blake was dragged back off his feet with over-full, fanged mouths slashing and gnashing by his face.

He struggled. The door and the safety it offered looked like they were shifting away in the opposite direction, slipping from his grasp. The Hounds had him fast, dragging at the clothes on his back.

Blake squirmed and flung out an arm, freeing it from the coat that had been protecting him but was now being torn to shreds. He struggled out of the Unseen Green as the Hounds gnashed and fought over it, tearing it to pieces. He dived for safety, crashing through the door.

As the moon reappeared in the sky, Blake glanced back to see the Hounds savaging what was left of the lab coat, biting at each other, attacking themselves, head to head to head. He smashed the door closed and held it there.

When the noise eventually died down, he heard another, altogether much more pleasing sound. 'Who is it?' Her voice came out of the shadows, afraid. 'What do you want?'

Blake crossed the small room into the moonlight falling in through the open window. 'I've come back again, Chimera,' he said.

'It's you!' she exclaimed. 'Oh, William!'

Fifty-Five

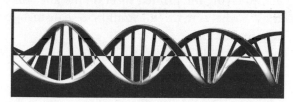

When the bell rang, he opened the front door and stood there for three or four moments without recognising her.

'Mr Newton,' she said.

He stalled for those few lingering moments.

'Mrs Gordon?' she said. 'Blake's head teacher?'

A million or more dreads were tumbling in at Blake's dad. He still had a headache and an unsettled stomach from the night before. As he faced the teacher, expecting more bad news, a pain stabbed into the corner of his left eye. He reached for his head automatically.

'Mrs Gordon,' he managed to say, still trying to gather his wits. 'Yes, yes. Of course. Won't you come in?'

He made tea for them both, taking a drink of water, calming himself before settling opposite her over the coffee table. She watched him closely as he poured, refusing sugar, accepting just a splash of milk. Mr Newton was feeling extremely uncomfortable, shifting in his seat, trying to think of what to say without simply asking outright what she was doing there so long after school had finished.

'Is Blake at home?' she said at last.

He glanced over his shoulder for a moment, as if to check the room. 'No,' he said. 'I'm not too sure where he is, at this moment.' Mr Newton felt ashamed under the inquisitive gaze of the head teacher. 'Perhaps I should make an appointment to come to the school with Blake to have a proper meeting with you?'

But she said nothing as she delved into her briefcase, bringing out a single sheet of paper. 'What I would very much like to know,' she said at last, laying the printed sheet on the low table next to their tea tray, 'is what is in this illustration to so disturb your son, as soon as he looked at it.'

Mr Newton studied the image, sitting down on the settee next to the teacher. 'Chimera?' he read. 'What is it?'

'The Chimera is a three-headed creature from the ancient Greek myths. I saw Blake's reaction to this picture today, and it was dramatic, to say the least.'

Blake's dad picked up the piece of paper. He had some vague recollections, a few snatches of some of the things Blake had said last night filtered through his head- and eye-aches. 'He said he had some proof,' he said, looking at Mrs Gordon.

'Proof?' she said. 'Proof of what?'

The goat-lion heads, the serpent tail tangled in a whirl in Mr Newton's over-flexing hands. 'Suddenly the world is full of monsters,' he said, with the doorbell ringing in his ears.

He looked up as, without a pause, the bell sounded out again and the door was thumped with such power and urgency that Mr Newton and the teacher both leapt into standing positions, facing each other.

'I don't think that's Blake,' Mrs Gordon said.

For a terrible instant, Blake's dad felt the blame that she, amongst so many others, would be laying at his feet. He felt, through the emergency of the pounding on the door, the poor parenting in the part he was playing in the losing of his son.

'That sounds like . . . ' the teacher said, tailing off.

She was going to say the police, he knew. She didn't say it, but Blake's dad was still expecting it, especially after such a series of rings and serious knocks on the front door.

But outside, he stood speechless once again, looking down on the girl he found on his doorstep, with her head juddering to one side. She held her arm in close to her, but still could not hide the twist to her young body.

'Are you Blake's dad?'

He looked about, to left and right of her, over her head, as if still expecting to see others there. He nodded.

'My name's Vanessa,' the girl said. 'And I need to speak to you, very urgently.'

Fifty-Six

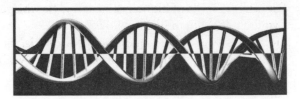

Blake's heart was still hammering, his hands shaking from the Head Hound attack. He was breathing heavily, trying to see Chimera through the gloom of her tiny, one-roomed house.

'Oh, William,' her bass-boom voice was coming at him, 'I'm so glad. I've been thinking about you.'

His heart was thumping. The Head Hounds had started it; now, looking at Chimera, excitement kept it going. Blake stood and waited, listening to the soft slap of her spread tail as she moved towards him. She came into view in the falling moonlight, eyes glistening, smile wide, milk teeth sparkling.

'I've been thinking about you, too,' he said.

She took his hand.

Blake leaned forward and kissed her on the cool cheek.

Chimera turned to him, her face practically in his. 'What was that?' she said.

'That?' Blake said. Then he realised – Chimera did not know. It had never happened to her before. 'That was a kiss,' he said.

'Kiss!' She smiled even more broadly. 'That's a kiss! I see! I've seen the word, but I've never had one. The Greencoats never kiss. There are so many wonderful words that no one's ever explained to me.'

'But I will,' Blake said. 'Chimera, I'll tell you everything I can. And I've been finding out so much.'

'And I want to understand, all of it. Like in your poems when you—'

'No!' he stopped her. 'That's the first thing. Chimera, my name's Blake. I'm called Blake Newton. I'm not William Blake.'

She blinked.

Blake felt it in the roots of his hair. 'I'm sorry,' he whispered.

'But, if you're not William Blake, who is?'

How did you answer such a question? 'No one is,' he said. 'William Blake was born about two hundred and fifty years ago. Nobody lives that long.'

'Don't they?'

'No, they don't. But people like him get remembered. Others are still interested in him, in what he had to say. They read what he wrote, like you do.'

'And you?'

'*Tyger, tyger, burning bright*,' he said. '*In the forests of the night*.'

She smiled. 'Blake Newton,' she said, savouring the words.

'Yes,' he smiled back at her. 'I am Blake. And I've come to help you – to stop what's been happening here.'

'You are Blake,' she beamed. 'Yes, you are.'

'I've come to stop what they're doing to you. They'll take all your blood and your stem cells and they'll make monsters of you for war purposes and for – for other things. They'll make experiments out of you. It's all one big military secret – and I've come to expose their plans.'

'And to take me to the Outerworld,' Chimera's eyes were sparkling, and her teeth. 'And I'll be free, like I've always dreamed, won't I, Blake? And you'll be there with me, won't you?'

Fifty-Seven

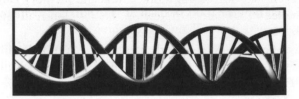

'Mrs Gordon!'

'Vanessa! What are you doing here?'

Blake's dad had almost stumbled into the girl as she stalled suddenly on seeing her head teacher. It looked as if Vanessa was having a change of heart as she turned round quickly.

'I've seen Blake,' she said, speaking directly to Blake's dad.

'We're waiting for him now,' the teacher's voice came.

But Vanessa's eyes were locked into Mr Newton's. 'There's something,' she said. She stopped.

'What is it?' Blake's dad tried to smile his encouragement towards her.

For a moment, the girl's eyes wavered, as if to indicate the presence of the teacher over her shoulder.

'Please,' Mr Newton said. 'Sit down, Vanessa. Take your time.'

But she sat quickly, clumsily thumping the little case she was carrying onto the table top. The cold tea cups clattered. 'Can I plug this in?' she asked as she pulled out the slim silver PC. 'I think the battery's about to go.'

'What is it, Vanessa?' Mrs Gordon was asking. 'What's going on?'

Blake's dad could see that the girl wasn't ready to answer. She was twitching, with her head dragged to one side, but her serious and determined eyes were fixed on him steadily. He took the mains lead and plugged in her laptop computer.

'I met Blake in the town centre,' Vanessa said, as the software went through its start-up procedure. 'He gave me this.' She was pulling something from her pocket and handing it to Blake's dad. 'It's broken,' she was saying. 'But I took the memory card and downloaded it. Sit here, Mr Newton. Look – you really need to see this.'

And as he sat beside her with Blake's broken mobile phone in his hand, Vanessa set her system to play a video recording. A picture came up. It was impossible to make out what it was. The camera began to steady. The images started to come into focus.

Mr Newton leaned into the screen. Three dogs seemed to spring from the computer at him. His head drew back in alarm.

'That's not three dogs!' Vanessa said.

Mr Newton's mouth fell open. 'Is that – is that—'

'Oh! My! God!' came Mrs Gordon's voice from behind them.

Fifty-Eight

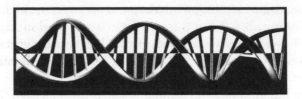

'I'll be free!' Chimera was exclaiming again. 'I'll have all the Outerworld to go to – we'll see it all, won't we, Blake? You'll show me everything out there, won't you?'

But Blake was trying to step away from her. For the first time he was being forced to think through what he was doing. He had no idea what freedom might be like for Chimera and for Ridley. She was happily slapping her tail against the wooden floor of her hut in her elation.

'The Outerworld,' she kept repeating. Her deep voice was dreamily far away.

For her, he could tell, the outside was a place of unending wonder in which William Blake's words had created a world in a grain of sand and an eternity in a flower. 'But they want to make weapons of war,' he said, trying to show her something of what the world was really like. 'Dod stands for Department of Defence . . . '

'Department of Defence? Defence from what?'

Blake had to work hard to make her understand. 'It doesn't necessarily mean just defence. It means attack, too.'

'Attack what? Why?'

But Blake did not have the words or the understanding to explain why wars kept happening, or why countries wanted always to develop secret arms and ever-mightier fighting forces. He'd never thought too much about it in the past. 'I only know,' he said, 'that the Department of Defence has research centres looking at all kinds of stuff. I mean, genetics!'

'But you've come to save us, haven't you?' Chimera blinked her wide, trusting eyes. 'I don't understand genetics,' she said, 'but it must be horrible. When you say it, it makes me feel so scared.'

'You were already scared, all of you! I've seen the effect when they take one of you away. I saw what happened to Bonnie and Bonno.'

She was staring at him, holding her breath. Her face looked tense, excited and perturbed at the same time. She had not exhaled for a long, long time.

Blake, on the other hand, was panting out his words, almost gasping over them. 'This place,' he said, 'I thought it was the entrance to hell, the Underworld. I thought you were all ghosts, demons, everyone insane. But not now. Now I think the insane ones are the demons like the Greencoats, doing what they do to you, and to Ridley and everyone else here. Now I know that the world – the Outerworld – has to see what's been going on here, for everyone's sake.'

Fifty-Nine

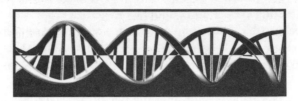

Vanessa turned up the sound on her laptop and a cow lowed sadly in a sing-song voice as rabbits scuttling round the feet of tall-walking dogs. A huge orang-utan sent signals through the computer to the outside world.

'Is he,' Mrs Gordon stammered, 'could he be – saying something?'

Blake's dad kept his silence.

'He's signing,' Vanessa said. 'Yes, he is – he's using some kind of sign language.'

The film changed. The screen darkened. In the shadows, lying out at full stretch, a very dark girl. She seemed to be waking from a deep, deep sleep. Her huge eyes flickered. They had no discernible iris or pupil. The camera moved steadily down her body, her slim, strong-looking body to ...

'Oh! My! God!'

But Blake's dad could not hear the teacher behind him. He could not see Vanessa looking round at Mrs Gordon's whitened face as the film came to a halt.

'How can this be?' the teacher was asking. 'It must be some kind of trick!'

'It isn't!' Blake's dad snapped at last, turning towards her. 'No trick! He tried to tell me.' He turned to Vanessa. 'But I wasn't listening. All that time!'

'Who would have believed it?' Vanessa said.

'But this means ... ' Mrs Gordon stammered again.

'Yes!' Blake's dad stood. He pointed at the screen. 'This means my son was telling the truth!'

He turned to Vanessa again. 'This means Blake wasn't lying to me!' he cried, picking her up and hugging her.

'But where is he now?' Mrs Gordon's voice came at them. 'Has he gone back there?' she asked, nodding at the notebook.

'Is it the research centre?' Blake's dad asked, as he put Vanessa down. 'Is that where this film was made?'

'It must be,' she said.

'The three-headed dogs – the mermaid!' He was back to pointing at the screen. 'All true!'

'We need to see him,' the teacher said. 'We need to find out exactly what's been going on, before we jump to any conclusions.'

'Jump to conclusions!' Blake's dad was jumping up and down. 'Look at it! That's a mermaid. You saw the dogs, the – what did you call them? – Cerberus? You saw them!'

'But what is he doing?' the teacher asked Vanessa. 'Where did you see him when he gave you this?'

'In the town centre, yesterday,' Vanessa said. 'But yes, I think he has gone back there.'

'Then we must call the police!' the teacher said.

'No!' Mr Newton stood firm. 'No, not the police! They're the ones who fitted him up with the drugs in the first place.'

'Ah, now!' Mrs Gordon said. 'You cannot go accusing—'

'Oh, yes I can!' Mr Newton interrupted. 'My son . . .' he said. 'How did I ever doubt him?'

'My husband,' Mrs Gordon was saying, 'happens to be a police officer and he would never—'

'Is he?' Mr Newton interrupted again. 'Here? In this town?'

'Well, no. But what you're suggesting – it implicates the whole of the police force in some kind of crime.'

'Not necessarily. Just those in charge. There are other, higher powers working here.'

'Blake was asking about Dod,' Vanessa said. 'About the Department of Defence.'

'And,' Mr Newton leapt, smacking his hands together, 'that's all Ministry of Defence land up there.'

'Oh, come, come,' said Mrs Gordon.

'No,' he continued. 'They said he'd stolen that bottle of stuff and that he'd drunk some. But he didn't seem – I mean, he was in trouble, yes. But not that. And I wondered why they hadn't called for a doctor, if he was supposed to have – if only I'd thought it through!'

'But you can't even be sure where he is, or what he's doing!'

'No, I can't be. But I trust him now. He's been there before, he always came back again.'

'But—'

'No buts!' he roared.

The teacher's face was ashen.

Mr Newton touched Vanessa on the shoulder to try to stop her trembling, wrongly thinking that he had frightened her.

'I will wait,' he said, his voice steady and sure, 'to see my son. I will listen to what he has to say and then I will decide what to do. If you'd like to leave me your home telephone number, Mrs Gordon, I will call you when I know exactly what is going to happen.'

'Shall I leave my computer here?' Vanessa volunteered.

'No ... no, thank you. This,' he said, picking up Blake's broken phone, 'is all I need. It's all in here.'

Mrs Gordon, shaking and pale, offered to give Vanessa a lift home.

'Thank you,' Blake's dad whispered to Vanessa at the front door. He watched her smile and walk away. She looked back and smiled once more as he closed the door gently behind them. He leaned back, placing a kiss against the shattered screen of the mobile.

Sixty

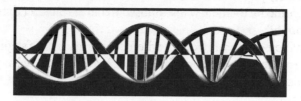

'But I can't walk that far,' Chimera was saying, looking down at herself, at her shifting, muscular tail, with regret. 'I can't make it over the grass like that.'

'Then Ridley will come too,' Blake said. 'We'll carry you between us. There are plenty of lab coats here.'

'But won't the Keepers see us?'

'We'll be really early, to meet the reporters outside. By the time the Greencoats realise what's going on, it'll be too late. The papers will be onto it.'

'And,' Chimera said, her face shining in the square of moonlight through the window, 'what does it mean, putting papers on it?'

Blake laughed gently. 'It means . . . it means everyone will find out about all this. It mean they'll see, because there'll be pictures of you, and of Ridley.'

'Then why not just take Ridley? He can run with you.'

Blake stalled for a moment. 'It has to be you, Chimera,' he said, 'because a picture of Ridley just won't do it. There are lots of pictures of orang-utans in the jungle and—'

'The jungle?' she said. 'Is that where Ridley would live, in the Outerworld?'

Blake said nothing. He could not picture the combed-through and scented orang-utan picking his way disdainfully through the dirt and damp of the rainforests of Borneo.

'And where would I live, Blake?'

She blinked at him as he maintained his silence. Her eyes were massive, with the little light coming into her hut. Blake could see the soft square of the window reflected back at him. He was trying to think quickly, to give Chimera something worth holding on to. 'You should be by the sea,' he said. 'You'd love learning to swim.'

'Would I?' she said. 'What makes you think so?'

Blake did not need to see her tail beside his legs in the deeper darkness out of the moonlight, with Chimera's skin shining like a wet seal and her web-fingered hand holding his. 'I just know,' he said.

She sighed. 'You know so much,' she exhaled, on the longest breath Blake had ever heard. 'You know so very much. I trust you, Blake,' she said sleepily, curling up by his side. 'I always have, from the moment I first saw you ... and I always will. Don't let them send me to Dod,' she whispered, with her tear-splashed face sea-water wet. 'Don't let them send me there.'

Blake touched her face, giving in to the wide sweep of her fearful eyes. 'I'm going to do everything I can,' he said.

'Just don't leave me,' she whispered. 'Just don't leave me now.'

Sixty-One

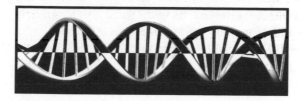

Blake couldn't help feeling that he should never have come back here. Chimera believed he was her saviour, returning to rescue her and carry her away. It all felt too much like a big mistake. Blake should have spoken to Vanessa for longer than he had, keeping calm, telling her everything. She would have helped him, he was sure of it. She and her friends.

As the moon went in behind a bank of cloud, Blake lost sight of everything, sitting alone in the complete darkness as Chimera slept. This was madness. Why was he here?

Now he had to face the question, Blake found he had no real answer. Out there, outside her village, Chimera would be nothing but a weird story in the gutter-press, a freak for everyone to gawk at.

This was wrong! It was not the way to stop the experiments. This was just a way of trying to clear his own name.

He unwrapped his hand from her web of fingers. Outside, a Head Hound growled once and then the hut fell into total silence. Blake stood, slowly, waiting to hear Chimera's exhalation again. It took a long, long time. Her lungs held onto the air for minutes at a time before releasing it. For all the girl-like looks of her upper half, inside she was as dissimilar to Blake as her tail was to his legs.

He stepped away, towards the door, taking down a fresh green lab coat from the hanger. Through the window, the moon made its reappearance in a clearing sky. Blake turned to go.

'Oh.' He heard her deep, deeply distressed voice behind him. 'Blake, if you went away from here now, if you left us, we'd be left with nothing again.'

His hand was reaching for the exit.

'Without you,' her voice came to him, 'nothing.'

He turned back to her.

Sixty-Two

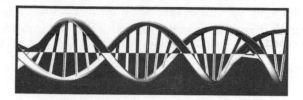

An alarm went off. He shot up onto his feet in an instant, shaking the sleep from his head, snatching up the trilling telephone receiver. 'Hello!' he bellowed.

'Mr Newton?'

He knew the voice, immediately. 'Vanessa?' he said. Outside the window, the street was still just lamp-lit. 'What time is it?'

'Is Blake back yet?' she was saying, ignoring his question.

He looked at his wristwatch. It was morning, but far too early to see the sun.

'Mr Newton!' Her voice across the landline sounded urgent and worried. 'The police have been here!'

'The police? To you? Why?'

'They came and took my computer away. They've taken all my files and my books, my CDs and DVDs, everything. But all they really wanted, I'm sure, was my computer.'

'But how – how did they know?'

'Mrs Gordon said her husband's a policeman,' Vanessa said.

'And she knew I'd kept the phone,' he said, as the street outside the window, still as dark as the streetlamps allowed, was suddenly lit, intermittently, by the flash of an approaching blue light.

'Vanessa, you're fantastic!' Mr Blake bellowed down the line.

Misplacing the house-phone in its cradle, he sent it clattering to the floor.

Blake's bed had not been slept in. His dad dashed into his room, pausing to touch the badly-arranged bedcovers. From there, he ran into his own room and picked up his coat from his bed. He was plunging downstairs when the first ring, the first rap, second ring and rap at the front door sounded out.

He did not stop. Out of the back door he ran and clambered over the fence into the garden behind his and out into the next street. Halfway to the town centre he slowed to a trot, then to a fast walk. He plunged his hands into his pockets against the cold.

All he had taken with him was Blake's broken camera phone. He had the clothes he had slept in, the coat he had grabbed in too much of a hurry. He had no headache, no stomach problems, no doubt and no fear. He also had no wallet.

Sixty-Three

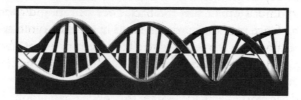

'I can't wait to get away from here,' Chimera was sighing.

Blake was looking out of the open window again, watching and waiting for the first signs of light. He came back and sat by Chimera. 'You're only going just outside,' he said, taking her hand. 'All we're going to do is walk round to the other side of the lab building.'

'Yes,' she breathed, 'where the paper people will be waiting for us. They'll be onto it then,' she said, using Blake's own words. 'They'll be onto it, just like you said, and then—'

'And then we'll have to wait and see,' he said, trying to sound stern. 'We don't know what the Greencoats are likely to do to prevent the papers,' he was saying, when a man's voice shouted outside.

'It's almost light,' Chimera said, looking away from him. 'At last.'

Blake jumped up again, with the yelping of the Head Hounds distracting his attention from her. He looked out through the first light at the Hounds being forced back into their tethering positions by men and women with sticks, all dressed in Unseen Green. 'As soon as the Hounds are tied,' Blake said, 'we must get to Ridley, as quickly as possible. We have to – you have to make him understand what we're going to do.'

'Ridley will want to get out,' she said, 'as much as I do.'

Blake's heart sank. 'But we'll only be just on the other side of the laboratory car park. We're not really going anywhere.'

'You don't think that's going anywhere?' she said. 'That's just because you've *been* everywhere – the Outerworld is all yours, Blake, and now we're going to have some of it, too. And Ridley's going to love it when those cameras are pointing at him and everyone looks at him the way he looks at himself in the mirror.'

Blake didn't say anything, with the sun coming up at his back against the shouts of the Keepers and the yelps of the Head Hounds.

'He's going to love it,' Chimera said, 'and so am I.'

'I only hope you're right,' Blake whispered, turning away from the heat of hope beaming from her face to the snap of frosted chain-lock tethering the Hounds to the ground.

Sixty-Four

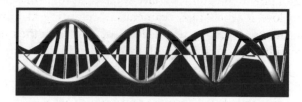

'Is it Blake?' the running club trainer's bleary-eyed face opened up at the sight of Blake's dad standing on his doorstep so early in the morning. 'What's happened to him?'

'Jimmy, I need to borrow your car!'

'My car? What for? Is Blake in trouble?'

'No – it isn't what we thought. I can't explain. There's no time. I – I've just got to sort it out, Jim. Give me your key, will you? I'll pay for—' Mr Newton had been just about to say that he would pay for any damage. 'I'll pay for the fuel I use. Please, Jimmy. We've done Blake down, all of us. We were wrong. I'll show you – I'll tell you all about it, later, when I can. But now I have to get somewhere, fast, and the pol—' No, he thought again, quickly, not the police. 'And the pol-*itest* thing I can say about my motor, is that it's junk. Please, Jim. I didn't know who else to ask.'

Mr Newton had to stand on the trainer's doorstep trying not to jump up and down. He clicked his fingers with fiery impatience as Jimmy turned away.

As soon as Jim returned with the dangling keys, Blake's dad snatched them from him and ran for his car parked outside on the street.

'What about insurance?' Jimmy was calling after him.

'I'll pay!' he yelled back. 'I'll pay anything – whatever it takes.'

Sixty-Five

The cow saw them and followed Blake and Chimera to Ridley's hut. Her head was poking through the window as Bonno opened the door for them. Ridley was filling out a far corner, giving his night tangles a rough brush through.

'Get them to leave,' Blake, nodding towards Bonno and the cow, was hissing at Chimera.

Chimera, busy signing at Ridley, appeared to be ignoring him on purpose.

'How are you?' Blake was trying to attract the Bonobo's attention. 'How are you feeling now, Bonno?'

But nobody seemed to want to hear him, whether they could understand him or not. Bonno was watching Ridley signing back to Chimera. Blake glanced towards them, at the smile on Chimera's face clumsily reflected by the stretch of Ridley's wide mouth.

'What are you saying to him?' Blake was asking, ignored once again. 'Chimera, what are you telling him?'

Ridley was grimacing into his hand mirror, brushing and spraying, grunting his approval to Bonno as Chimera made more signs close to his distracted face.

'Chimera!' Blake almost shouted, demanding her attention by hauling at her shoulder. 'Just tell him we have to go, now, just the three of us.' He held out the green lab coats he was carrying. 'We need to get Ridley's body covered in Unseen Green. But we need to do it right now, before the Keepers come.'

He turned as he heard the door crashing closed behind Bonno. 'Where's he going?' he said. 'What's Bonno doing?'

Chimera was still signing wildly at Ridley, who was swinging from one side of his house to the other, gathering his things together.

'No!' Blake cried out. 'Ridley, you won't need hairbrushes. No perfume. Tell him Chimera. We're only going just outside.'

But she was directing him to look for her things, the books he always looked after for her.

'Chimera!' Blake dragged at her again. 'Leave everything. We'll be back. We're only going to . . . '

He tailed off. There was a noise coming from outside. The cow moved away from the window as Blake neared, as he looked out and saw them.

The little streets were full of villagers: Boons, Spiders, dogs and pets and pigs . . . every one squealing and squeaking excitedly, with one white-eyed, frantic bonobo chimpanzee at their head, urging them all along.

Sixty-Six

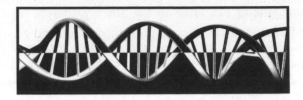

The low sun, which had been shining into his eyes, was blocked out by the army lorries lumbering ahead of him. Mr Newton was forced to drive more slowly, with so much military hardware out on manoeuvres on the approach to the moor.

Overhead, he spotted a huge green Chinook helicopter hanging over the moor on its giant twin blades.

Once, Mr Newton pulled out to try to overtake the truck in front of him. He quickly swung back in, as soon as he saw how long the convoy up ahead was. There was a similarly long line of cars making their way in the opposite direction, away from the moor. He tapped on his steering wheel, 'Come on. Come on.'

But the truck in front slowed still further as the convoy came to a halt. As it did, a police car swung in, pulling up in front of Mr Newton's borrowed car. A policeman got out, putting on his hat.

'What's happening?' Mr Newton asked, winding down his window. 'What's going on?'

'Excuse me, sir,' the officer leaned in. 'Can you tell me where you're going, please?'

'I'm going to the town,' Blake's dad said, thinking quickly that it was best not to mention the research laboratories.

'I'm sorry, sir,' the policeman said. Behind him, the trucks were taking off again. 'I'm going to have to ask you to turn back.'

'But why? What's happened? My son is over there, and I must—'

'The whole area is being evacuated,' the policeman said.

'Evacuated? Why?'

'This is Ministry of Defence land. There has been an accident.'

'What kind of accident?'

'I really couldn't say. But you must turn round and get off the moor.'

'When did it happen, this *accident*? Some time last night?' He was wondering, looking up into the officer's face, what time Mrs Gordon would have been telling her husband, the senior policeman, about the images on Vanessa's computer.

'I'm not at liberty to say, sir,' the man said. 'In fact, I don't have any further information. I can only tell you that this area of the moor has been designated under military control, and that everyone will be swiftly evacuated. Please, sir, turn back and don't worry about your son, he will be perfectly safe.'

'He'll be safe, will he?' Mr Newton was still asking, as the policeman stopped the on-coming evacuee vehicles to allow him to turn the car.

Sixty-Seven

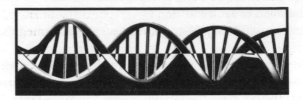

'What are they doing?' Blake gasped, staring out at the villagers.

Bonno had brought them all together, grouping them about the entrance to Ridley's house. The chimpanzee had his arms raised. His white eyes and teeth were flashing as he spoke, as he screeched out at those surrounding him.

'Stop him!' Blake was shouting out above Bonno's hideous wails. 'The Greencoats will see! Chimera, Ridley – make him stop.'

But the orang-utan was moving towards the window, still taking a last languorous look into his hand mirror. He took a glance outside.

'Ridley!' Blake tried to speak to him. 'Do something! Chimera, make him do something!'

'What's he saying, Ridley?' she asked, peering past Ridley to look out at Bonno as the villagers let out a collective cry, a roar of excitement.

Ridley started to sign at Chimera.

'Blake has come,' she translated, to Blake, although she did not look at him. 'He has come to rescue us!'

'What?' Blake cried, making for the door. 'What's he saying that for?'

'He has come with his great words from Chimera's book,' she said, halting Blake in his tracks. 'He has come to rescue us from Dod and take us to the Outerworld.'

'No!' Blake tried to say.

But Chimera went on: 'Blake knows all things! He knows all

about the Outerworld – Blake tells us it is not all Greencoats there. We have to go, all of us!'

Blake ran to the door, throwing it wide.

'Dod will take us all if we don't . . . ' He heard Chimera repeating the meaning of Ridley's signs at his back. He slammed the door on her.

The villagers looked his way, a multitude of faces, eyes, arms and hands, legs and feet, fingers, claws, hooves and pads. So different they were, with so many species condensed into the one space, with a single, over-hopeful expression on their nervous, near-frightened faces.

Sixty-Eight

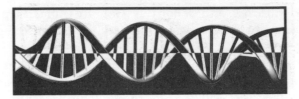

Driving back the other way, Mr Newton looked into his rear-view mirror and saw a line of vehicles following him along the road. Twenty minutes or so further on, he pulled over into a little lay-by. He sat and watched the cars and vans and trucks driving past. But there was no end to them – a whole town-full of people on the move, driven away from their homes.

He turned on the car radio.

'... *a military spokesman has assured us that the danger is very, very slight, from such a low level of nuclear radiation ...*'

'Radiation?' he whispered to himself. Outside, the convoy of cars continued unabated.

'... *merely a precaution to evacuate the area until the extent of the threat has been thoroughly assessed. The public has been asked to keep clear of the Great Western Moor and its surrounding towns and villages. There is an emergency telephone number ...*'

Mr Newton switched off the radio and got out of the car. He scanned the sky. Another huge army helicopter chopped its way across the unbroken morning blue.

'Radiation be damned!' he said, pocketing the car keys and setting off away from the road across the flat spongy plain of the moor.

Sixty-Nine

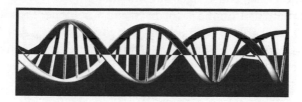

Blake ran back into Ridley's house. 'Chimera! Make them stop.'
He moved aside to allow Ridley out.

Chimera slapped across into the doorway. 'They all want to be
saved,' she said.

'But not like this!' Blake was shouting. 'Ridley! Bring them
down! Now! Down!'

And then he stood horrified as the great orang-utan, seemingly
misunderstanding his words, turned and launched himself,
barging against the shuddering pole.

Blake turned to Chimera with a look of desperation.

'This is wrong!' she said. 'We've all lost friends to Dod. No one
ever wanted to be sent there.'

Behind them, Ridley took the pole in his hands and gave it an
almighty shove. It shifted slightly. Ridley pulled it back the other
way. It tilted more. The massively powerful orang-utan gave
another huge push and Boons seemed to drop from the sky,
landing on the ground with a light patter and a squeal, running
off in all directions.

'They believe in you,' Blake heard Chimera saying.

His heart was sinking still further as Ridley pulled again. He
roared with the effort. In response, a gang of hysterically wailing
Boons were with him, pulling up the pole from its foundations.

At last it gave, with bits of camera smashing down as the top
of the pole landed first, the other end still held by Ridley and the
Boons.

The Spiders were leaping for joy. The pigs were running in excited circles. Bonno was roaring at Ridley, who started to make elaborately exaggerated signs at Chimera.

She translated Bonno's words: 'It must be done. Let's not be afraid – Blake is here with us! We have to break our way into the labs. Everyone here will be rescued. But we have to go in this way. We'll never get past the Head Hounds anywhere else. The labs – it's our only way!'

Seventy

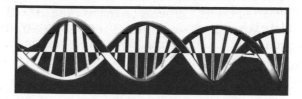

But Blake stood back, unable to move. He watched the over-excited villagers grabbing at the felled pole. They started to run. The Head Hounds looked up as they approached. For a few moments there was hardly any response.

Not until Bonno, in the lead, was practically eye to eye with the nearest, the twelve eyes on the six heads of the two closest Hounds, did the reaction start. As Bonno and the others drove forward, faster now, faster still, the Hounds' heads roared and the great black brute bodies leapt.

Crash! The chains held firm as the vast brutes were dragged out of the air, falling to the ground, thrashing.

The pole-drivers barrelled through between the writhing, spitting bodies. All down the line of chains the other Hounds were infected by hysteria. The whole village was in uproar.

The blunt top of the pole made first contact, crashing into the metal-reinforced wooden double doors. They splintered and shuddered. The shock of impact was transmitted back along the pole and every strong body vibrated with it.

They gasped.

'Move back!' Blake screamed, running to them. He had no choice but help them. It shouldn't have been happening like this, but it was and there was nothing Blake could do about it other than try to co-ordinate their efforts. 'When I say. Back further – get ready – go!'

And they ran once more through the drool-spit tunnel of

howling Hounds' heads and again were smashed to a splintery halt.

'Once more!' shouted Blake, to be heard but barely over the outraged roars of crazed Cerberus on chains close left and right.

'Go! Go! Go!' Blake flowed forward at the front with Bonno, with Ridley right behind, gritting against the next splinter-smash and shudder of the doors.

This time, one door was broken in two from bottom to top, falling through into the corridor behind. Bonno ran on, kicking the surviving half-door and the other one wide. He stood roaring back at the Head Hounds, his fists in the air.

Blake stood with him, watching.

On the village side of the Cerberus barrier the villagers jumped and somersaulted, turning in tight circles, squealing. Among them, still and certain, Chimera looked at Blake with eyes full of admiration and joy.

Just inside the building, Blake saw the trolley in the corridor. It was the one he had come across in the lift that first time, the day of his arrival here. He realised at that moment that this was how the feed must be brought down from the room with all the fruit in the research centre. He knew, also, that it would never be coming down again.

He dragged on the handle, pulling the trolley out between the hysterical Hounds as they bit at its edges, towards the triumphant villagers. 'Here!' he yelled, trying to signal to Ridley. 'Help me.'

Chimera came to meet him. She kissed his cheek.

Blake gave no response. 'We've got no choice now,' he was saying, pointing to the four-wheeled hand truck. 'We'll have to take you out on this.'

Chimera put her arm around his shoulders. He tried to pick her up. She was shockingly heavy – much more so than Blake had been expecting. He made a frantic signal out to Ridley. Together they raised her and placed her carefully in the centre of the moveable platform.

Bonno was still standing in the broken doorway flinging his arms, gnashing his teeth.

'There's enough room to get everyone between the Head Hounds,' Chimera shouted over the never-ending noise.

'Everyone?' Blake said. 'Surely not everyone?'

But nobody was listening to him. Bonno rushed through to help Blake drag Chimera's new wheels towards the smashed-open doors. The Hounds were flying at the edges of the trolley, teeth smashing down on wood and metal in a gnash of splinter grind, wooden and metallic at the same time.

But the Hounds could not stop them. Blake and Bonno pulled Chimera through, stopping her just inside the building at the beginning of the long corridor. Ridley remained on the other side of the ring of Hounds to hold back the hysterical villagers.

Blake dashed back outside to help Ridley guide the other villagers through the sparse gap between the braying multi-heads gnashing towards them. The Boons and the Spiders came flying through, dashing for the safety of the space beyond the open double doors. Bonno was shoving the dogs with their pets, bowling them along and trying to guide the terrified pigs as they squirmed and squeaked.

But the pigs were too frightened and tried to turn back. One was caught, and then another, bitten in the fearful face and dragged into the bloody mash of three salivating mouths.

The other pigs squealed and ran as the unlucky ones were pulled to pieces in a quick splash of blood and devoured on the spot in three unequal parts. The Head Hounds hardly stopped to draw breath, swallowing and driving forward immediately with reddened gums and thin pig-skin-draped teeth.

Seventy-One

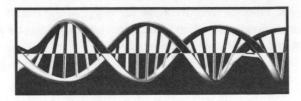

Now the corridor on the other side of the Hounds was frantic and chaotic with milling villagers. The only one left outside, as usual, was the cow. She turned and tried to run away, tripping delicately on her high hooves along the road. 'Leave her!' Blake was shouting after Bonno and Ridley as they chased her. They turned her around. Bonno held her head and pulled, while Ridley pushed from behind.

'Let her go!' Blake tried to order them.

But through the ranks of the gnashing Hounds they forced her, with barely a hair's breadth either side. Her flanks were grazed by outstretched claws, one side, the other. She swayed and baulked, scratched and caught, bleeding from several slashes, her blood driving the Head Hounds into even greater kill-crazy frenzies.

At last they pulled and shoved her in through the open double-door entry. Blake had to clear the other villagers, shepherding them back to make way for the cow and Ridley behind her. The cow was slipping awkwardly on the smooth tiled floor inside.

Ridley appeared, squeezing past the weeping cow's rounded bleeding belly as Bonno leapt through the gap between her back and the ceiling. Ridley signed to Chimera, she relayed a message to Blake.

He could not hear a thing above the noise of the crowded tunnel. Ridley had to silence them all.

Chimera spoke. 'But what if they let them go?' she said.

Blake looked puzzled. 'Let them go – the Head Hounds, you

mean? How? There are no Keepers down here to do it.'

'They have to come down to chain them up,' Chimera said. 'They've never had to be there when the Hounds are let loose.'

'But how . . . ' Blake was saying, still puzzled.

His face changed then – as soon as he heard it.

A thunk, and then a clanking clatter – the sound of an automatic release mechanism, followed by the dropping of many chains.

Followed by a ghastly silence.

Seventy-Two

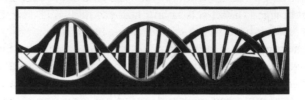

A moment was as long as the silence lasted. That was all the time it took for the first of the Hounds to round the corner and roar, its three heads joined almost immediately by another three, and another, as the guardians of the Underworld piled into the corridor space.

The terrified villagers were streaming away in the other direction along the tunnel. Bonno and Ridley roared back at the Hounds. But the entrance was black with them.

Blake dragged them back. Chimera was helpless on the trolley, rigid with fear. Blake started to pull on the handle. There was too much weight. He needed Ridley.

The cow, between them and the Head Hounds, was slipping and tripping, trying to turn so that she could run. All the other villagers looked like a moving sea of fur, falling over each other, rolling forward in the only direction they could go.

'Ridley!' Blake screamed. 'Ridley! Take the handle! Take Chimera!'

One of the Hounds had leapt onto the back of the distraught cow. Another joined it instantly. Her confused face was looking towards Blake, begging his help.

But now the Hounds were piling in, one after the other, pressing from behind. Blake tried to pull the cow, jamming her across the corridor. He was staring into her eyes. They were tearing at her back, at her far flank.

Ridley and Bonno had got the trolley shifting along at an

incredible rate now. But if Blake were to help the cow, if he moved her round so that she could run, he'd be clearing the way for the Hounds to give chase to everyone else. And no matter how fast Ridley dragged the wheeled platform, it would still be far, far too slow.

Blake hugged the cow's face. He could just hear her. She was singing. She was still standing, blocking the entire corridor with the savage Hounds scraping and biting at her from one side. Their claws appeared over and round her, dragging at her, as if scrabbling through her body.

The entrance to the corridor was blocked, dark with the force of so many bodies trying to get through. Outside, Blake knew, the scent-frenzied Hounds would be tearing each other to bits to try and take a bite out of the cow. He had to let her go. He had no choice. Her song was already drawing to a close and her life about to ebb away. Blake did not like to think of what a state her big body was in, on the other side.

She sank to the knees of her front legs, with the back still jammed upright. The space above her was packed tight with Head Hounds.

'Keep going!' Blake turned away, shouting at the villagers. He knew he'd have to find an escape. More Hounds were on their way and everything would be devoured.

Up ahead, he could just make out the door of the little lift as lights came on automatically.

Blake squeezed past the trolley and ran to the lift door. He pushed again and again at the call button. All round him Spiders were jumping, Boons screaming as they looked back towards the augmenting rage and roar of the Hounds.

'Come on! Come on!' Blake shouted. But he knew now that the lift was never going to respond. He pulled open the other door to the tiny winding staircase.

'Through here!' he screamed unnecessarily. The villagers were already dashing in, a constant stream of them climbing the stairs on feet and on hands. The tall dogs were on all fours now, dragging their pets on leads with them. The thin pigs were like pink strips of flowing flesh pressed writhing close to the wall.

Last to make it to the opening was Chimera, with Ridley and

Bonno pulling her along. Blake held the door for them to drag Chimera through on her trolley.

He took a final look down the long corridor. The cow, still jammed in position in the far distance, was fading away. Her head hit the floor, nose first, with her final song finished and at an end.

Blake screwed his eyes closed and turned away, slamming the door closed behind him. When he could bring himself to look again, he was confronted by faces, ahead and above, winding upwards round and round the stairwell, the village-eyes all looking down on him. He peered through the gloom on the ill-lit staircase at shocked, silenced and fearful expressions, in all their various types and forms.

'What have we done?' Blake breathed heavily.

PART THREE

The
Outerworld

Seventy-Three

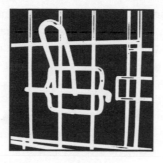

Blake dashed upstairs with Bonno scuttling at his heels. At the top, he found the next door locked. Blake charged against it with his shoulder. He was as hefty as he'd ever been, but the wood was too solid. He bounced back.

Bonno raged at the door, as ineffective as Blake at breaking through. Blake peered down the stairwell past the dogs and Spiders and pigs to where the Boons were assisting Chimera up the stairs, followed by Ridley straining against the weight of the sideways-on wheeled platform.

Blake went back down and helped Ridley thump the trolley all the way to the top. Bonno showed Ridley the locked door, which was nowhere near as thick or as strong as the entrance's double-doors downstairs. Ridley went at it, running head first.

Watching him, Blake had to grit his teeth in anticipation. It looked as though Ridley was going to try to butt the thing open. But at the last moment, his long arms came out and he just pushed his way through. The door flew aside, split from top to bottom and Ridley was diving through the gap into the storeroom, into bunches of bananas and piles of apples, sending fruit falling to the floor all round him.

In a moment the Spiders were in there gorging themselves, closely followed by hungry Boons. Bonno stood looking about, searching for something. Blake turned back and helped Chimera through the open door. Picking up a whole cold fish that had been thawing on the side ready for her breakfast, she threw it into the air and caught it as she did before, swallowing the thing down in one go.

Ridley had a mouth crammed with all kinds of exotic fruit. Blake picked a single banana from a huge hanging bunch and went through into the room with all the animal cages.

It was empty. Only a scattering of sawdust across the shelves and the floor showed any trace of what had been held here. Blake looked about, astonished.

Bonno appeared at his right hand, scanning the empty shelves with light, hopeful eyes. The bonobo chimpanzee was breathing in great lungfuls, sucking up any scents left behind. Blake watched him as he sniffed his way round the room, with grains of sawdust spattered across his nose.

Suddenly, Bonno seemed to be on to something. Blake saw the renewed concentration in his face. Bonno dashed towards the door at the other end of the room. His mouth opened and all his teeth showed.

A shot rang out. There were screams, both Bonobo and human. Blake ran through the open door as Bonno leapt and another rifle flashed.

There were two men with guns, others unarmed. Bonno was still jumping. Blake dived for the man levelling his reloaded firearm at Bonno. He grabbed the gun and wrenched it out of the man's grip. He went for the other gun as the second armed man fumbled to reload the tranquilliser dart. Gun and tranquillisers hit the floor.

Bonno was shrieking, rushing at the two men as they grappled with Blake. Others picked up the empty rifles and used them to swipe at Bonno.

'Out!' a man shouted orders. 'Everyone! Out now! Bring him with you!'

He was wearing a blue suit. Blake had seen that flickering face before – on the moor, standing in the on-off lights of the arresting police cars, watching him with a satisfied look on his flickering face.

Now that same suited man was pointing at Blake as the other two men dragged his arms backwards. Bonno was still trying to get to him, but the rifle butts were flying, one catching him on the side. Bonno screeched in angry pain.

'No!' Blake heard a girl screaming.

He was suddenly aware of another face he recognised. The young lab-assistant, the school-trip guide, was over by the refrigerator, crying out when Bonno was struck.

'Get him out the door!' the man shouted over the girl's head. Blake looked at her, and she at him. 'Get him out, now!'

A red explosion burst through the door and roared in their faces. In a single moment, Ridley had swung across the room and swatted the two men from Blake's back.

Then it was as if the vacant doorway was giving birth to more and more diverse creatures, spitting Spiders and Boons through the opening.

'Out! All of you!' the suited man was railing, picking up the Keepers from the floor and shoving them through the other exit door.

Blake felt the floor under his feet again as Ridley released him gently.

The lab-guide stood by the open refrigerator, her arms full of phials and bottles of serums and drugs, wearing a look of stark shock and puzzlement.

But the man wearing his dark suit of authority was ushering the Keepers and the lab staff out of the exit. 'Now! You!' he bellowed at the girl. He turned his red face to Blake. 'You too!' he yapped.

'Wait!' shouted Blake, as the girl went to move away under orders. 'Don't go! We've got something important to show you.'

'Who are you?' she asked.

'Out!' the man roared again at the girl, as if to prevent her questions.

Blake indicated Ridley and a long red arm stretched out and halted the man in his tracks.

'Chimera!' Blake called through the back doorway.

The puzzled girl stared at Blake.

The man took another look at Ridley. 'I'm ordering you,' he said through gritted teeth, threatening his subordinate, 'I'm ordering you to get out, right now.'

'Stay!' said Blake. Through the outer room, he could hear the rhythmic slap of the seal tail across the empty sawdust floor. 'You must see this place for what it is,' Blake said to the guide.

As she appeared in the doorway, Blake held out his hand as if to introduce her. 'Chimera, tell them, tell her,' he said, looking at the guide, 'what we're doing here.'

Chimera's attention was drawn to the blue suit and the rage in the face of the man wearing it. She glanced at Ridley.

He nodded quickly, just once.

'We want our freedom,' she said, just prior to the sound of the glass bottles and jars falling from the girl's arms and smashing on the floor at her feet.

Seventy-Four

All the way round the periphery fencing the army trucks with thick and knobbly cross-country tyres had been driven into place, spaced at irregular intervals. On guard, every here and there, armed personnel in battle fatigues had been positioned to form a loose cordon round the Ministry of Defence land.

Blake's dad kept going, creeping round outside the thin green-and-brown army line of soldiers, keeping just enough distance to see and not be seen. His leg muscles were screaming at him for running so far bent almost double, across such hostile terrain. Every few steps he would stumble and fall, getting wetter every time.

But now he had chosen his spot. There was a dip in the ground, a kind of little valley that led all the way up to the fence. The undergrowth was different, tucked away from the cruel, relentless moorland wind. It was longer and softer. Blake's dad had been able to crawl on his belly along the dry ground under these plants until he was close enough to one of the lorries to hear the voices of the soldiers either side.

Soaked to the skin on his back, Mr Newton did everything he could to keep his front dry and warm. If not for that, he thought he might have died of hypothermia.

So he crouched shivering, peering through the ferns at the army lorry driver sitting in his cab drinking tea, waiting and waiting for his moment to come.

Seventy-Five

The girl looked in horror from Chimera to the man in the dark blue suit, to Chimera again. Her eyes were bulging in her shocked pale face. Her mouth was moving but no words would come out.

'You didn't know,' Blake said to the girl, 'did you? Nobody knows – except ... '

'Out!' the man stepped towards the girl.

'Ridley,' Chimera said.

The orang-utan flicked the suit back against the wall.

'She – she can talk?' the lab assistant was glaring, wide-eyed with wonder at Chimera.

Blake nodded. 'Speak to her yourself.'

Bonno was moving closer to the guide.

'You know what it is I'm saying?' she asked, stepping back from the burning white heat of the bonobo's stare.

'Yes,' Chimera said. 'I understand you.'

The girl gasped again. Blake went to her, to help hold her steady.

'Enough now!' the suited man said, still pinned to the spot by the close proximity of the giant red body in front of him. 'We must leave – immediately!'

'Yes,' Blake said, but he directed what he was saying to the lab girl. 'Take what you've seen with you – tell everyone. Go to the papers – tell them the truth!'

'The truth?' the man said. 'You want the truth, you young fool?

The truth is, all these – these creatures would all be dead if not for this place.'

'If not for your military research, you mean,' Blake said.

'Military?' said the guide.

'This place is backed by the Ministry of Defence,' Blake told her, 'and linked with the Department of Defence research centres—'

'Enough!' The man tried to move again.

Ridley snapped to, his fur flowing, covering the ministry-blue of the suit, as if to smother the man inside it. Bonno twitched by the guide's side.

'Let him go, Ridley,' Blake said.

Ridley glanced at Chimera, who made a simple sign for him. He stood back, his red fur falling loosely at ease, with one of his huge hands reaching over and falling on the shoulder of the shuddering bonobo.

'He reads sign language!' the girl said. 'He does understand! He knows!'

'And so do you, now,' said Blake.

'You know nothing!' the ministry man snapped. 'Any of you! You fools!'

'I know that the government has allowed this to happen,' Blake said. 'They've let people like you,' he turned to the guide, 'start to mix up human and animal genes.'

'No,' the guide shook, 'they're all destroyed before they can develop into—'

'That's not true,' Blake said, glancing at Chimera.

The guide said nothing, but continued to stare at the man, demanding an answer. For a long, long while everybody stood waiting. Dogs on two legs leading their guinea-pigs, Boons and Spiders and skinny pigs were filing through from the other room, gathering like evidence against the blue-suited authority of the man.

He crumbled, eventually. 'All governments,' he said, 'except the British, have forbidden the splicing of human and animal DNA in embryos for stem cell research. But did you seriously think that an administration passing a law could ever prevent these experiments? That they would never be taken to their ultimate conclusion?' He looked about at the array of faces staring back at him. 'All we've done is offer a safe haven for the chimeras, for the abominations, the real victims of . . . '

'Abominations like me?' Chimera said.

Blake watched the guide's whitened face looking around the room.

'Yes, just like you,' the man spoke to Chimera.

'You knew,' the guide said to him. 'You knew, didn't you, that she . . . that Chimera could speak. You knew how intelligent, how – human she was!'

'Of course I knew! Why did you think we kept her here, with people like you, barely out of university, just out of school, doing as you were told like good little children, never asking any probing questions.'

'That's why the Keepers were always so cruel,' Chimera said, 'wasn't it? To keep us, to keep the whole thing in place?'

'Very well,' the man said smiling condescendingly at Chimera. 'You've had your little say. Now it's time to end this.'

'No!' the guide said. 'What have we really been doing here? Offering sanctuary? I know that's not true. Research into DNA manipulation for medical purposes?'

'Yes,' the man said.

'No!' said Blake. 'Military.'

'But I thought,' the guide said, still looking at the man, 'that these things came from the illegal labs they closed down in South America?'

'They did,' the man said.

'All of them?' Blake said.

The guide glanced his way. 'How many did they breed?' she asked. 'And how many do you have here?' She, along with the villagers, was still glaring at the ministry man.

'Look,' he was shouting back at the accusation in their faces, 'if we didn't do it, others would. If some tin-pot science student stuck up a river in the rainforest can make Cerberus dogs, what other kinds of monsters will come slouching out of the jungle?'

'But is that what we were doing all the time,' the guide said, 'creating monsters?'

'The whole world will, sooner or later. We have to be first, if we are to have any bargaining power. We have to research, whether it be nuclear arms, chemical or biological ones – it doesn't matter what people think. How do you imagine that we have negotiated treaties on the non-proliferation of weapons of mass destruction? By not having any? Don't be absurd.

'And where did you think the most significant advances in science and technology and medicine really came from? They come from the creativity dedicated to peace – and peace is always a question of balance. On the one hand, there is co-operation, while on the other, the one that promises threat, has to be a fist. The greatest technological developments ever seen on the face of the earth came as a direct result of the research into the exploration of space. And what was that for? It's strategic, militarily, like nuclear weapons. Like *all* weapons. They'll always be manufactured, we have no choice. But, with the proper political negotiations, provided that we are given enough bargaining leverage, they will never be deployed. Maintaining the balance is a process, that's all. And you,' he said, pointing at the guide, 'will have to learn to embrace the process if you're ever to make the grade as a scientist.'

Seventy-Six

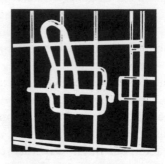

Blake never knew if Bonno had understood any of the words of the argument, or if he had just gathered the gist – but the effect, either way, was to send the little bonobo into a violent screeching rage, flying at the face of the man, wrapping his arms and legs round the man's head, biting viciously on his nose until Blake and Ridley could get to him to start to drag him off. The man collapsed, roaring in pain with the bonobo chimpanzee fixed to his face.

As soon as Blake and Ridley dragged Bonno back, the Keepers returned in force, clattering through the door with metal batons, thrashing at the wailing villagers, one man drawing back his stick to strike Chimera. The young guide let out a shriek, half scream, half shout to stop.

But Ridley was there, flying at the attacker, flinging out one great hard hand and sending him spinning back into the wall.

Blake tried to restrain Bonno as the ministry man, bleeding red onto the official blue of his suit, his nose and the side of his face torn, staggered to take hold of the guide. 'Out! Now!' he was raging but confused, turning to look for the exit door.

The guide tried to break away but Blake took the opportunity to grasp her other arm. He found himself being stretched apart, the frenetic bonobo in one hand, the struggling guide in the other.

Ridley loped over and picked up Bonno, fixing him under one arm, slapping the sticks from the grips of the surprised keepers with his free hand.

Blake wrenched the guide from the ministry man. 'You've seen them for what they are now,' he said to her. 'Take what you know. Let the world see what's been going on here.'

The ministry man, lurching forward again, gripped her shoulder.

'But what will happen?' the guide turned on him. 'What will happen to them?'

'They will be taken care of,' the man said, dragging her towards the door.

'What do you mean?' she asked, pulling him back. 'You can't kill them!'

'No, I can't!' he snapped. 'But they'll destroy themselves. Come on. Right now! Everybody, out!' he ordered the largely disarmed Keepers.

The man's bloodied face fixed onto Blake's. 'You should leave here too, right now, with us. I'm giving you just this one chance.' He stared into Blake's eyes. 'One chance to leave,' he said. 'Before it's too late.'

Blake took a quick look back at Chimera. 'Destroy themselves?' he said. He shook his head. 'Never. I'll not leave them.'

The man smiled cruelly. He wiped the blood from his nose. 'Your choice,' he said, turning, striding out through the door, shoving the young guide towards the exit from the building.

Silence surrounded the shocked and frightened villagers. Bonno was lowered to the floor at Ridley's side. Chimera was watched Blake closely as he walked to the window and looked out.

Down in the car park the research staff and the Keepers were being loaded into people carriers and police cars with flashing lights. The girl appeared, still held fast by one elbow. Blake watched the man from the ministry say something to a uniformed officer. The policeman took the girl from him and pushed her, on her own, into the back of one of the squad cars.

Blake knew then that she'd never get the chance to speak. He could not see her any longer, but knew that, one way or another, she'd be discredited as he had been, and no one would see her for what she was, or listen to anything she said.

And then he was exchanging looks with the man in his

authoritative dark suit. Blake was looking down as he looked up, mopping his face with a bloodied handkerchief.

'Why don't you send in the police?' Blake whispered, as if asking him directly.

But the man, giving another quick cruel grin, turned away and got into the back of a big black limousine with his own driver in the front. As his car pulled away, everyone else, the lab staff, the other drivers, the police, slamming closed their vehicle doors, disappeared in a fluster of flashing lights. Nobody was left outside.

'Why don't you just come in and capture us?' Blake went on asking, as if they were all still out there.

'Oh, no!' he heard Chimera exclaiming, by his side. 'Bonno – no!'

Blake followed her index finder, looking down on frantic Bonno as he, still searching for his bonobo love, chased after the cars as if Bonnie was only just now being taken from him.

'Bonno!' Blake tried to shout through the glass.

Blake and the villagers watched Ridley gaining on and quickly recapturing the little bonobo, turning with him struggling in his arms, making his way back down the road towards the research centre.

'But I thought the journalists were going to be out there?' Blake heard Chimera saying by his side. 'I thought they were going to take pictures of us.'

'And so they are,' Blake said, watching the cameras on the deserted security posts focusing in on the caring orang-utan cradling the all-too-human pain of a desperately grieving chimpanzee in his arms.

Seventy-Seven

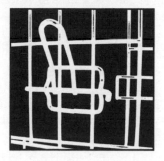

Blake held the telephone receiver to his ear with the newspaper reporter's card in his hand, but all he could get was a very high frequency screech that seemed to be coming from somewhere else. 'Hello?' he said.

The line was dead. Blake threw the phone down, but the high-pitched sound continued, broke off, then started again. 'What *is* that noise?' he asked.

The villagers were beginning to file out of the door, moving towards the exit.

Chimera was still looking out of the window, peering down into the car park below. 'It's Bonno – he's standing there, in the Outerworld. He's calling us all.' She was staring into the far distance beyond the razor wire at the periphery of the research centre grounds. 'The Outerworld,' she said. 'There's nothing to stop us now.'

Blake rushed to her. 'We should wait here, for the reporters. Don't go anywhere. You don't know what might happen out there.'

The villagers were quickly disappearing behind him, the first of them scampering across the car park. Bonno was in full swing, chattering away, showing his teeth, flashing his white eyes. He was constantly pointing up and over the surrounding hills in the direction the line of cars had taken.

'Don't listen to him,' Blake said to Chimera. 'Bonno's hurt. He still thinks he'll be able to find Bonnie somewhere.'

But Chimera's eyes were fixed far away into the future she had dreamed of for so long.

Blake was calling Ridley back in. 'Don't let them go,' he said. 'Ridley – listen to me!'

But Bonno's screech was drawing them on, his pain translated into passion as the villager's felt freedom for the very first time.

'Dod's still here,' Chimera said to Blake, as Ridley helped her towards the stairs. 'The Keepers will come and take us back.'

Blake was left speechless, following them into the car park where the villagers were already beginning to set out, trekking up the road between the hills.

Ridley made a series of hand signals to Chimera. She turned to Blake. 'I'm going to need the cart,' she said. 'Ridley wants to know if you'll help him bring it out. Will you help him, Blake?'

He hesitated. He let out a great sigh. 'Call the others back,' he said. 'Let's keep together, at least. Tell them to stay with me. I know where the nearest town is. We'll go there, and ... and ... '

'And we'll be saved from Dod,' Chimera said.

Blake glanced at the pained, bestial expression of the passionate bonobo urging the villagers on. 'I hope so,' Blake said. 'I really do hope so.'

Seventy-Eight

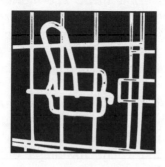

Just a short while later, Chimera was perched on the platform ready to be moved. Blake had a dozen spare tranquilliser darts in a box, with one of the rifles loaded in his hands. Bonno called the villagers to a kind of order, leading them through the car park. Chimera, with Blake at her side like a guard with a gun, was being pulled by Ridley and pushed by the Boons. Spiders tumbled along at the feet of upright marching dogs and their scuttling pets. The rear was taken up by four pigs, all that were left now, stick thin and bright pink in the morning sun.

'Keep together!' Blake called again and again to the scattering Spiders and cringing pigs.

Bonno marched ahead, bursting with determination, towards the nearest town on the moor. The road they followed swept round the bend and up the hill.

'There are no cars,' Blake said quietly to himself.

Every so often a huge, double-rotor helicopter would pass overhead. The first time it happened, Chimera cried out that they should hide. The villagers had scattered, but there was no cover to be had on the low-lying moor.

Blake watched another fly over, very high up. Then all was silence, with just the wind whistling across the open grasslands. He ran forward alone, climbing the next hill to get the earliest look over at the next stage of their journey. Bonno came after him, but Blake did not speak to him. They stood side by side, human with bonobo, silent in the whistling wind, gazing down on the gathered rooftops of the little town.

Nothing moved below them. Mid-morning, and no town sounds, no traffic movement, not a single soul to be spotted between the houses or the rows of shops. And no more helicopters. Blake looked back again at the movement of the straggling band of villagers. Bonno waved them on, urging them forward.

Bonno forged ahead while Blake turned to watch the others as they gazed in awe. The town was not big, nor its buildings particularly imposing, but to the villagers it all must have appeared massive and stately, crowding in on them like a world full of palaces and kings.

'Who lives here?' Chimera asked Blake.

'Just keep going,' he said, pointing at Bonno pounding ever forward towards the centre of town. 'You'll soon see. We're not quite there yet.'

But they were. Already they were walking, swinging, scuttling and riding on the trolley down the street between the glassy shop fronts. The villagers were agog, peering into the displays, pointing, speaking in low, whispering voices. They gazed everywhere in reverence, their mouths open.

'This,' said Chimera to Blake, her husky voice even lower than usual, 'is wonderful! The Outerworld – it's better than I could ever have imagined. It is so like a – so like a miracle!'

Blake looked, too. He'd been to this little town many times in the past, with his mum and dad, and then once with just his dad. But now it was as if he'd never seen it before. Now he seemed to be looking at everything through the eyes of the villagers, or at least through Chimera's.

Chimera reached out for him, taking his hand. 'What's happened here?' she said, glancing away from him at the deserted town square that Ridley was wheeling her into. 'Where have they all gone?'

Blake pulled his hand from hers. 'I wish I knew,' he said, watching Bonno leaping from place to place, for ever searching.

But there was nothing to find here but empty, silent buildings and a lonely town square with a stony obelisk, a war memorial set in its centre. Only bits and pieces of trash were left to show any sign of recent occupation, old crisp packets and plastic bottles and drinks cans erupting from the litter bins. A polythene bag blew across the square as the villagers stood and stared.

Blake watched the discarded supermarket carrier skitter over the flagstones and halt, caught on one corner of a strange black box by the tall war memorial. For a few seconds the bag flapped there, filled with air, one handle snagged on the sharp corner of the box.

The polythene carrier flew off, as if away from Blake as he stepped closer. 'What's this?' he said.

He bent down, looking at his reflection in the uppermost shiny surface of the box. He placed his hands on either side. It was not big, but it was very heavy. Blake tried to pick it up. He could barely move it.

Bonno and the villagers were watching him expectantly, as if he knew what this thing was and what he was going to do with it. 'Ridley,' he called the orang utan over. 'See if you can lift this thing,' he said, miming what he wanted him to do.

Blake stood back, watching Ridley's reflection in the opaque surfaces as he loped nearer with the little bonobo by his side. He could see the long red fur blowing in the wind. He saw the massive arms stretching forward.

And then, with a huge grunt, the reflection of Ridley flew away in a mass of shocked red and wide open, multi-toothed mouth, with his hands clasped over his ears.

Seventy-Nine

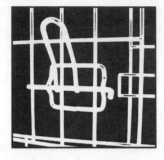

Ridley staggered back against the other villagers. Bonno was still jumping into the air, shrieking. Blake could only stand and wonder what had happened.

Then he saw that whatever it was, everyone but he and Chimera were squirming in agony, falling to the ground, or leaping from it, spinning away from the blank black box with hands or forefeet to ears or thrashing heads. Ridley fell down, his precious clean and scented fur knotting together under him on the dusty ground.

Blake ran to Ridley. As he did, Ridley stopped. He sat up. Blake glanced at the other villagers as they started to calm. 'What was it, Ridley? What's wrong?'

He followed the flow of the long, long arm leading to the index finger pointing at the inert black box. Bonno was already leaping onto it, attacking it with his teeth as if it were the nose of another ministry man.

'What is it?' Blake looked to Chimera, as Ridley signed at her.

'A sound,' she said. 'A terrible noise came – as if from there. It was like – like a stabbing in the ears ... '

She stopped mid-sentence, halted by Ridley as he leapt from the ground into the air, as Bonno and the Boons and Spiders, dogs and rabbits, guinea-pigs and pigs ran round and round, trying to escape the needle pierce inside their heads. To all four corners of the town square they scattered, hiding behind stone pillars, diving round corners, disappearing along the many small side streets.

Soon only Blake was left standing there, with Chimera perched on her stationary platform. He kicked the box. The force of his foot moved it, just slightly, but damaged his toe more than anything.

'We can't hear it, you and I,' said Chimera, looking about.

'Everything else can, though,' Blake said, collapsing back into a public seat, trying to hug his foot.

'Yes,' Chimera said, 'everything else can. Blake,' she continued, in almost a whisper, 'Why does it do it, that box – why does it make such a sound? And what else can hear it?'

Blake looked up. The little town was surrounded by hills. Between them, over the rooftops, he thought he might have seen something. Or perhaps he just felt it. He stood, peering over, trying to see or feel it move again.

'It's nothing,' he said, but without looking at Chimera. 'It's just a box. Like a music centre or something. Or something like – like the thing they have on aeroplanes, the black box that – that ... '

The indestructible flight recorder from an aeroplane left sitting in the centre of a little town on the moors, transmitting ... transmitting!

'What kind of signal – what for?' Blake was asking, staring now into the perfectly shiny surfaces, deeply opaque, reflecting his thrust-forward face, the lined-up rows of shops around the square.

'I don't like it,' Chimera was saying. 'Blake, I really don't. It's for something, it has to be. Something's coming, Blake, I can feel it.'

'Yes,' said Blake, knowing, feeling what Chimera felt, looking for another movement, something showing in the surfaces of the box. 'Yes, I can feel it, too.'

He turned to look at the shops instead of their reflection. There was nothing more to see. He turned back again. The box sat squarely, perfectly immovable – although now it did not appear so fixed. Along one side it seemed to shimmer, to flicker and then to writhe.

'Blake!' he heard Chimera say.

But his eyes were fixed onto the faces that were appearing, one after the other reflected on the side of the box; faces he knew, or at least had seen, printed out in the form of a terrible, nightmare internet image.

'Blake!' Chimera screamed.

Eighty

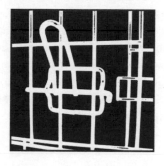

For a moment, Blake and Chimera shared what felt like a last look. It passed so quickly and with such finality, giving way to a new era, like the time leading up to and away from a disastrous accident.

As at the moment of unavoidable impact, Blake's gaze had to swing away to confront the change. From the gap between two buildings, filling up the street space, the bringer of disaster stepped, writhed, slunk and crept and lunged, moving forward as if in several separate ways, but all at once.

The air was altered. Blake felt it. He heard the use to which oxygen was being put, sustaining so huge a beast. It appeared in three parts, serpentine dragon hissing head first, devil-goat horn next, just before and above snarling darting lion eyes. It came through the gap as though in three pieces, but kept on coming, kept on, kept on coming. Snake and goat and lion head turning this way and that, three very different types of eyes were peering out at the one shocked world. The huge supporting body stepped with horrifying heaviness against the cracking paving stones. Lion-bodied, but bigger, vaster, heavier, with dragon-serpent tail, the devil-head of fiercesome goat and slant-eyed, thick-maned lion, it turned, all three faces fully head-on staring, breathing over Blake.

Standing by the black box, he stared up and up and up, one face piled on top of the other over him, gigantic, making midget lap-dogs of the dead Head Hounds. Hissed, groaned and growled at, Blake stood within the stench of its hot, evil exhalations, trying not to faint. Trying to move away. Trying not to cry out.

One head tilted one way, the next the other, the third twisted and turned, lion, goat, dragon. The mouths came open. Blake looked into the heat haze of throat-black interiors as they rose over and above him, teeth and tongues, more fiercesomely multi-headed and over twice the size of any Hound, manufactured by genetic manipulation out of the imagination of a crazed mind from ancient Greek times. Alive in the here and now, the giant thrived. The Legend. The Myth-Monster.

The Chimera

Eighty-One

Chimera screamed. The sound boomed from deep within her frightened throat.

The three disparate heads of the beast snapped away, focusing as one. It lurched forward as she flapped in terror on the platform of her trolley.

'No!' Blake yelled.

But the beast had turned. Its massive thumping feet rumbled through the ground with every step it made.

Chimera sank back on her platform.

The beast's three heads moved in turn now, two always fixed on Chimera, one then another then the third taking a look round, ever aware of its surroundings, able to look all ways at once.

Chimera let out another cry.

Blake saw the tension in the lion body as it crouched. 'Hey!' he shouted, flapping his arms. One head looked his way.

The snake face thrashed hissing in his direction, pulling back on the goat and lion lunge attack at the front.

Blake ran to the stone obelisk and snatched up the gun. But the snake head had joined with the other two again, looming over Chimera. Shuffling backwards, she fell from the platform onto the ground as the nightmare beast roared towards her, gnashing at the air.

'Hey! HEY!' Blake yelled. 'HERE!'

And he raised the gun and shot the vast lion body in the side. Three fearsome heads turned, three sounds, one scream.

The sound alone was enough to knock Blake off his feet. As big as a ploughing Shire-horse but even broader and more powerful, a single dart was never going to send this monster to sleep.

All three heads swung into action, raging, turning, squirming, shrill-bleating and hot with hiss, roaring, spitting and flinging at Blake. He had to fall away, diving behind the solid stone of the war memorial, dropping the gun.

With one swipe of a massive forepaw, the whole monument to dead soldiers toppled and fell. The metal spike from the top of it clanked and sparked as it broke up on hitting the street.

Blake ran over to the shop fronts. There were more stone pillars here, holding up a roof covering the open pavement. The whole thing came crashing down almost onto Blake's head as he darted through, and disappeared down a small side street.

He chanced a glance back to ensure that the giant was still going for him and had not turned back to Chimera. But he needn't have looked. Blake could feel its breath, hot and serpentine, goat and lion exhaling, meat-eating and murderous on the back of his neck, all down his legs. He ran harder, faster. He was quick.

Blake cried out with the strain of running so fast. The ancient monster of the legends was gaining ground, even restrained as it was by its smash, smash, smashing motion. Every thumping step it took thudded down with a shudder that Blake was sure he could feel through the soles of his own fast flying feet.

He was lucky. The lane was so narrow that the beast was slowed by its flanks grazing against the buildings, cracking through into all the little shops on either side.

The monster was squeezed tight between these face-to-face buildings. And Blake knew this place. His mother had loved these little lanes, all the cafes and quaint shops that were being so systematically shattered now by the beast's steady advancement. Blake remembered that this road was a dead end. Further ahead, not too far, was a tiny alley on the right, nothing more than a narrow gap between the buildings. All he had to do was get there first and dive through, leaving this clumsy lumbering giant wedged tight at the end, unable to advance or turn round. By the time it worked its way back out, edging in reverse back down the broken aisle, Blake and the villagers would be all the way out of town.

He was thinking quickly, with his legs not unlike the Supermouse blur beneath him, when something hit him. *Wham!* A lump of dislodged wood had landed Blake between the shoulder blades.

As he went down, curling into a ball, Blake was aware of the Outerworld turning over him in a moving mass of diverse gnashing teeth from what should have been three entirely separate species. Over and over he went, springing back onto his feet after the double somersault.

The hissing huge serpent slithered just over his head. Almost onto his left shoulder, the horned devil champed, while on his right the greatest ever lion roared. Over and above him, all round him, the Myth-Monster.

It would have torn him, head from split, bisected body, had Blake not at that very moment been able to fling himself sideways, falling through into what he hoped would be the safety of the little narrow alleyway. On the ground again, all he saw was the open mouth of the serpent as it slanted through the gap at him. Filling up the space behind it, two other furious faces, one on top of the other, raged from the shoulders of a trapped giant lion body.

Blake kicked upwards and caught the hissing serpent with his heel as he backward-rolled away. He jumped up, just out of reach of all three contrasting but uniformly vicious heads. Now he could stand and look for a few moments. The enclosed creature raged and spat, trying to lunge through at him, attempting to turn. Its screaming hissing spitting wrath was almost overwhelming.

Blake stood gasping in the heat of its outraged breath as, writhing savagely, unable to go forward or back, it started to claw and to bite its way upwards. Blake stepped back as the Myth-Monster began to rise, clambering up the close walls, knocking the corners off buildings, screeching and hissing its way to the crumbling, collapsing rooftops.

At last Blake found the strength to turn around and run away, with the giant crashing above. He dashed to the end of the alley, turning into one of the streets that would lead him back to the square. Blake could still hear the roaring rage of the beast smashing through the crumbling rooftops. There came a huge crash, a rumble, another roar.

Blake ran harder to get back to Chimera and Ridley. Now he knew there would be no time to get everyone out of the town. He'd have to think of something else, to find a way of exterminating this thing, before it destroyed and digested them all.

Eighty-Two

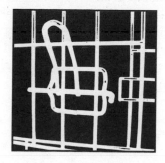

Bonno, Ridley and the villagers were helping Chimera return to her perch on the platform as Blake burst back into the square.

'We'll never outrun it!' Blake called, startling them all. Find somewhere to hide! Now!'

Blake ran and collected the gun and the other tranquilliser darts in their box where they had fallen on the ground.

Ridley and Bonno helped the Boons shove Chimera into a side street. There, Blake kicked at the glass door of a shut-up shop. It did not give way. But it shattered when Ridley hit it, allowing them to push Chimera through, hiding her and most of the villagers in the dim interior.

'Tell them,' Blake said to Chimera, 'tell them what I'm saying.'

They were shaking their heads, as if in refusal. But in reality they were trying to shake out the shrill stab of the black box noise that Blake could tell had started up again.

'Listen to me!' Blake roared. 'Listen hard, everyone! That thing's coming back, the—' Its name was on his lips . . .

'What it is, Blake?' she said, the mermaid mixture of human and animal cells, the chimera inheritor of this monster's name. 'What kind of thing it is?'

'It's a . . . it's a biological weapon,' he said. 'There's an ancient legend – but we don't have the time. It's coming here! We don't stand a chance against it unless we act together. Bonno, Ridley, we do it, or we die. It's as simple as that.'

Eighty-Three

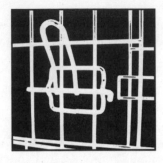

As it moved with heavy thumping steps down the lanes, its snake head snapped from side to side, the snarling, gnashing lion and goat biting lumps out of the air. Every so often it lashed out, breaking glass, wood, brick and stone.

It stamped thudding into the square where it still emitted the high frequency seek and attack signal. The Myth-Monster halted. The lion head came up, elevating the horned slash of the goat into the sway of the snake. The triple captive species appeared at war with one another, all three now roaring, bleating savagely, hissing and viper-spitting.

Blake, hidden behind one of the stone pillars left standing under a section of undamaged pedestrian walkway, peeked round and pointed his gun. The beast was so huge this close up he could not miss. He pulled the trigger again. One giant forepaw of the lion swept Blake's protective pillar aside.

Exposed, he aimed and shot upwards with the tranquilliser gun, hitting the lion's chest dead centre. The giant reared and raged. It screamed, its three atonally pitched voices rattling Blake's teeth in his head.

Ridley darted past him, flowing red. The raging beast above them lashed out, snapping three times after him. Bonno ran in the opposite direction. The monster could not make up its minds which way to go.

Blake reloaded the gun. He shot again as Ridley swept away

behind the broken war memorial and Bonno dived into a smashed-open, empty doorway.

More Boons cried out from the roofs nearby. The rearing lion body carried all three heads upwards.

As Blake shot once more, one of the Boons was grabbed by the flailing serpent. In a moment, the Boon's life left it, gone in a spray of red that splattered across the square. Other dispersed Boons were calling from every vantage point. 'Hey! HEY!'

The screaming snake went for them, with steam streaming from its nostrils. At the same time, the lion and the goat were wildly enmaddened by the agile, leaping Spiders.

Blake had reloaded and he shot again straight away. The monster's lion feet, dragged in every direction by three thrashing heads, staggered slightly. It appeared to be slowing. Blake had shot it with enough tranquilliser to kill a small herd of buffalo. He had only the two darts left in the box. It *had* to be enough.

Although the beast's thrashings were slowing now, its rage was relentless. Still the debris flew as lumps were being broken from the surrounding buildings of the square.

Blake saw an injured Spider staggering away, bleeding profusely from its head. He watched as it fell and died. Blake paused, his hand poised over the loading chamber of the rifle. Just a little way away, the Spider lay, with its open damaged head in full view. Blake slammed the last of the darts into the gun.

Turning to fire, the serpent's dragon face was there, in his own. It struck, still as quick as any snake, despite the tranquilliser in its blood.

In an instant, Blake's determination to kill the creature was dispersed by fear as the devil snake bit and snapped by his ear, catching onto the hood of his jacket. One moment and his feet were firm, the next lifted, with the gun clattering to the ground and Blake was being carried as if on hiss, on slither and slide, up into the serpent-slippery air.

Eighty-Four

He cried out. The Boons called back, 'HEY! HEY!'

From up there, Blake had to see the brute body of the giant beast, its long sharp goat's horns, its coarse mangy mane. The terror of what was happening seemed to slow everything down for Blake. He had time to examine all the dreadful details of the creature that had him clamped into one of it sets of drooling jaws. The slit-irised goat's head snapped at him, champing under his feet. Below that, the lion turned slowly, its mouth crunching, molar on molar as it barely missed a Spider here, as it caught and crushed a struggling Boon there.

Ridley was a blur of raging red below, his fur shifting so very, very beautifully.

Blake wanted to reach for him, to hold onto him for strength and safety. But then he could not see him any more. The sky rushed towards him as he was thrust upwards, the ground approaching fast as he was thrown down again, jerked to a bouncing halt, shaken from side to side.

He was confused, disoriented. Fear had given way to something greater. Dread and then horror had subsided until all there was left inside him was – loss.

The beast, the legend was winning; it was going to destroy them all. Their ill-conceived little adventure was at an end. And now all Blake wanted was to see Chimera once more. Just once more. It was as if time had halted, suspended on this moment as

Blake was left dangling way above the cracked and breaking ground. He had failed.

The dragon serpent thrashed him from one side of the square to the other. But to Blake, again the motion had slowed, showing him in horrific detail the crunch and the spurt of Boon and Spider blood below. The sky moved over Blake's head, across his face like the majestic dome of the heavens circling mightily above. His limbs felt weightless now, only his head heavy with sorrow.

Then, from one distant corner of his eye, Blake caught sight of a patch of moving darkness, like a little black cloud. Something had been launched from one of the roofs nearby, landing with a thump onto the head of the serpent. Blake seemed to awaken at the momentary sight, struggling to look upwards, catching just a glimpse of a bonobo chimpanzee tearing mad and gouging at the blank black, forever-open snake's eyes.

Eighty-Five

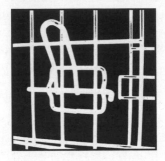

The jaws came apart and Blake was falling. Above him, the huge serpent swung away, hiss-screeching against the primate fingers jammed into its eye sockets; below the cracked flagstones of the town square. Everything still seemed so slowed down, gracefully revolving, shifting away, approaching with gentle calm until ...

Crunch!

The hard ground leapt at him in the very last millisecond, sweeping up under his feet and forcing his legs up to his chin.

Wham! His knees cracked him under the lower jaw and threw him backwards.

Thump! With the pavement pillowing the back of his head, the concrete causing the flash of an internal light illuminating the whole of Blake's brain.

Then the light went out with the darkening of the sky. A great eclipse came like an opening lion's mouth gaping – no! The lion's jaws stretched and Blake was caught inside the gap between them. His screaming senses had all just switched back on in a moment of violent contact, leaving now no time to cry or to cry out with so many and such vast teeth surrounding him.

An almighty surge of fear seemed to lift him, spinning Blake on his back. His legs kicked and propelled him backwards at an incredible rate.

But as the giant jaws clumped gnashing next to his ear, as Blake felt the wind created by that brutal bite, he heard the Boons calling at his collar in their near-human voices. He knew then that it was they who had pulled him clear. It was the funny Boons now being impaled on thrashing goat horn, sacrificing themselves to save Blake.

He leapt up. The lion's face turned towards him, viciously open-mouthed and slant-eyed. Blake leapt over the fallen war memorial. He saw the metal spike from the top of the obelisk, where it had broken off and fallen into the road.

'Help me!' he screamed at the terrified few surviving Boons. 'Here!' he indicated to them.

Flailing over them, the slowing serpent shook and spat, still trying to dislodge the crazed bonobo scratching at its open eye sockets, biting down onto its head. The snake's hiss gushed out into the cold air like steam, or smoke, as if the furious dragon really did breathe fire.

'Lift it!' screamed Blake, heaving against the heavy metal spike on the ground. He indicated that the terrified Boons should take hold of the shaft with him, as they had held the fallen observation pole back in the village. But now they were too few, too weak.

Then the spike came up in Blake's hands as if it suddenly weighed nothing. Ridley was back by Blake's side, fighting with him.

The chimera was slowing now, with the flow of tranquilliser making its way into its bloodstream. Blake and Ridley ran with the Boons, out from the protection of the stone obelisk, under the smoke-streaming snake's head.

Blake roared with Ridley, leading them side-on to the lion body as it shook its three heads. 'Now!' Blake screamed. 'RIGHT NOW!'

And they ran at the side of the lion as they had run at the escape door through the Head Hounds. Then, they had crashed against the metal reinforced wooden doors; now they plunged through flesh towards the huge heart of the impossible Myth-Monster. Blake ran them hard. The metal spike was sharp. But the lion muscles and its sinews were strong.

Three raging heads thrashed, crying out in pain. Blake and Ridley fell back with the Boons, tumbling away from that hurt, hurtful noise. They scattered as the lion, the goat, the dragon screeched long and loud enough to make the buildings shudder as if in an earthquake.

Blake saw Bonno slip and start to fall. But the snake was thrashing in agony and did not notice the bonobo sliding down and running away.

As Bonno dashed from the thrash and the enraged cries of three-in-one, Blake ran to him. He pointed. Ridley was still right by him, pointing too. They had to go back.

They had to finish this. Now – right now.

Eighty-Six

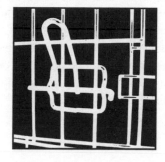

Together they launched forward, driving the spike further through the ribs into the beast's lion heart. But Blake and Bonno were knocked sideways as the giant twisted in agony, sent spinning by the protruding metal shaft.

All he could do was observe as Ridley held on and held on to the mast until at last the thrash of the beast slowed just enough ...

He needed a single second, or even less. In that moment as the Myth-Monster took a huge staggering breath, Ridley was down, his feet on the ground and he was all lunge.

Blake looked over dizzily. He saw Ridley. He saw the beautiful and flowing orang-utan gain the ground, wedge himself, take hold of the suspended spike and shove.

Ridley drove it home. He stabbed the abomination through its single heart and ran as the whole thing came down about him.

Bonno dashed to help drive the spike further in, to ensure the dark heart within the thing had burst apart. But Ridley had done it.

The lion collapsed, its lower jaw striking with a smash onto the pavement, the goat head dropping down on top. Blake stood next to Ridley and watched as the serpent head fell last of all, winding down to the ground with a falling hiss as if it was finally deflating.

Eighty-Seven

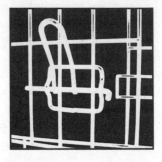

That was the last breath of the Myth-Monster, leaking away with the remains of its life. All round Blake and Ridley and Bonno, frightened-faced Spiders and Boons were re-appearing. There were few, too few of them left now.

But a great silence descended as the survivor villagers stood and looked with awe and dreadful wonder at the great beast.

Bonno moved first. He went searching, as always, as if for his lost love, finding only more frightened Spiders hiding in crevices.

Then Blake turned to Ridley, as Ridley turned to him. Their eyes met and held. They were both too shocked and saddened by the deaths of so many Boons and Spiders to celebrate their victory. But they *were* victorious.

They had done it, together.

And together as equals they walked away from the square to the broken-open shop where Chimera and the others, the pigs and the dogs, were hidden.

Chimera gasped with relief when she saw them. 'What happened? Are you all right? Is anyone hurt?'

But Blake and Ridley were able to say or sign nothing. Between them, they manoeuvred Chimera on her platform from the broken shop and led the dogs and few cringing pigs back into the town square.

There they stood and surveyed the body of the great beast in silence, while Bonno searched and Spiders and Boons tried to gather together what was left of the remains of torn Spiders and Boons.

Blake watched Chimera's expression of pain as one of the Boons in mourning dashed to the lion body and tried to drive in the fatal spike still further. It made no difference, not now. The Boon scuttled to Chimera's side. Placing a hand on its head as it buried its face in her side, she looked back at Blake.

'This,' she said, pointing at the huge lion face with foam and blood dripping slowly from its mouth. 'And this,' she pointed at the goat's dead snarl, its sharp, stone-hard horns. 'And this,' finally to the head of the snake, its open black, angry eyes. 'All this – this whole thing – this is what Dod would make of me, isn't it?'

Blake nodded, just slightly. He still could not find any words to say. He needed to drink something. His legs were going wobbly under him.

'Then we were right to escape,' she said. 'And you – only you could have rescued us.'

Ridley appeared at Blake's side.

Blake wetted his cracking lips with a barely moistened tongue. 'Chimera, I—'

But her face stopped him. Her expression had changed, and changed again. Fear, to horror, to terror. 'On, no!' she rasped. 'Oh, Blake!'

Blake turned. He saw it. There was no missing it – the fear, the horror, the terror. In every direction they were there – more, four more beasts approaching. Lion, goat, snake came clambering, stamping into view, evil, devil-eyed, drooling and hissing, filling Blake's stunned senses, homing in on the town, legends, giant walking myths, monsters descending from the hills.

Blake felt Ridley by his side. 'I've got no more tranquillisers,' Blake managed to say at last. He turned to look at the orang-utan.

All the other villagers were there, every one looking towards Blake. Chimera too, looking and looking at him.

There was nothing he could do.

'Run,' he said simply.

But nobody moved. They stood staring, as Blake did, at terror approaching, listening to the hiss-roars, the frantic bleats as the creatures crunched through the streets and over the rooftops towards them.

'Oh, Blake,' Chimera managed to say.

Ridley was pulling at the handle of Chimera's trolley, trying to drag her back to her hiding place.

'No!' Blake shouted. 'Not that way!'

But there was too much noise as the four giants roared and raged and hiss-screamed into the town, attracted by the black calling box and then Ridley's defiant call. The villagers were in disarray, confused and disoriented. They scattered in complete confusion, with the pigs swiftest on foot, running away on their delicate trotters, tearing up the streets for their lives, squealing in panic, they were snapped up and ripped, splatter-shaken to death. The sound was fearful. Beast screeches at feed, enraged roars, acid hisses and the last shrill pig squeaks hit hard in the centre of town.

'There's nothing more I can do!' Blake was shouting.

The Spiders were scattering across the roofs. They were being picked off by high-sailing serpents, snake-swallowed whole.

Chimera had taken hold of Blake, dragging at him in panic. The Boons and some few of the Spiders were dashing back and forth, or running round in circles, pulling at their own fur in sheer terror. The upright dogs stood shivering with their squeaking pets in their thin arms.

The roar-snarl-hiss of rage was rolling ever closer. Chimera held Blake too tightly for him to push or pull the trolley anywhere. Ridley dragged them all round the square, looking for a way out. There was none.

They could feel the air altering round them. The town was being trashed, with crashes growing closer as the roars grew louder, the whole in-coming disaster augmenting, condensing.

Chimera was holding harder and harder onto Blake.

'I should never have come back,' Blake was saying, although no one could hear him. 'Why did I ever think I could do any good?'

But the first of the beasts burst into the square, rumbling in fast and grinding to a sudden, rollicking halt, surprising everyone with its size and shape, the sound it made and the blue smoke billowing from behind.

Eighty-Eight

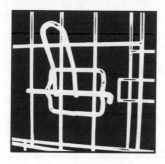

Blake ran back to the rear of the vehicle to help Ridley load Chimera on board.

Blake heard a man's voice shouting out through the window at the front of the lorry, but his words were lost under the window-rattling roars of the beasts as the first and then the second of the monsters arrived, bursting from between the buildings with stretched faces and ready, open mouths.

Blake stumbled, trying to lift one of the fear-rigid dogs. Bonno appeared and leapt on board and he and a few of the Boons were reaching down from the back of the truck and dragging Blake up by the back of his collar, while Ridley held Chimera firmly in one place.

The dogs were flinging their guinea-pig pets on board before leaping to try to get away. A few made it. Most were taken as the monsters flew at them, three and four appearing, crowding in from all round the town. The square was full of heads and slashing, grinding teeth. Rabbits were being snapped up, dogs broken in two, in three and devoured.

Everyone on the platform jolted, hanging onto the metal slats at the sides, as the truck started off, accelerating madly in a smokescreen of half-burnt diesel. Blake was still holding hard to the dog he'd been trying to save. Ridley was keeping a tight grip on Blake, dragging him up.

They were all thrown violently sideways as the Myth-Monster beasts ran in, crashing at the side of the vehicle. Blake tried to turn, with Ridley pulling him up under the armpits. He looked back at the dog he thought he had rescued.

Blake had to let it go. He held only the top half. Everything else was gone.

The truck slammed into one of the giant creatures. Its face must have been broken by the impact, but still it did not stop. Acceleration was always being delayed by another bone-cracking crash, another raging roar, another hissing snake face appearing, only to be punched away by the hard hand of the huge orang-utan.

Chimera was slipping, Spiders leaping and Boons screeching. Ridley had positioned himself at the very back of the truck, preventing anyone else sliding off into the snapping jaws following too closely behind.

Bonno leapt and scratched and Ridley swiped, lashing out again and again.

But still the different heads kept coming. The truck lurched and rolled as it was driven into another mountainous creature body. Everyone on the back could hear the metal panels crunching, folding. The roars of pain and outrage were so savage the Boons were trying to put their hands over their ears, falling and rolling from side to side, prevented from falling off only by the flat metal bars running from front to rear. Between the slats, bending them, trying to drive through them, faces with evil eyes threw forward for the kill.

Blake was trying to keep a hold on Chimera's smooth and strangely waxy skin when the biggest crunch came. The lorry lifted, lurched, throwing everyone. Even Ridley stumbled, dragging himself away from the teeth snapping after him. He swung onto the metal cross-members connecting the slats from one side of the truck to the other.

Snake faces sneered in at the villagers, taking a Spider, a Boon, another Spider before Ridley could fight them away.

The engine was screaming. The blue smoke bellowed out at the back. Blake stuck his head through the bent side bars and caught a glimpse of the lion face gnawing away at the thick rubber of the front tyre, its whole body stuck under the lorry.

But the lorry seemed to step over the obstruction, tossing its passengers from one side to the other, finally accelerating away from the chaos. The shocked survivors looked back in silence at warring Myth-Monsters, blood crazed, with lion attacking goat now, goat lunging after serpent, serpent snapping at everything that moved. As they made their way along the road and up the hill, the centre of town looked to be moving, writhing.

Eighty-Nine

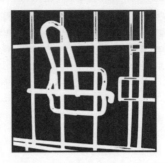

The battered truck was listing to one side as it trundled down the other side of the hill out of sight of the town, the platform under them vibrating wildly as they turned off the road onto a dirt track across the heather.

Blake's teeth kept clumping together as he peered out through the twisted slats. In the distance he spotted a group of what looked like large agricultural buildings, or some kind of small factory complex.

Hardly able to bring himself to look round at the diminished numbers of the villagers, Blake kept his eyes fixed on their destination until the lorry turned off the track into the yard between the barns and workshops, stopping at the biggest wood-and-metal-built building.

Blake leapt from the back and pushed open a pair of vast clanging doors and the lorry drove forward against its burst front tyre and the engine was turned off.

As the doors were shoved together again, darkness closed in. The vehicle lights snapped on and the driver's door of the truck swung open.

And Blake was suddenly standing face to face with his father.

There began a long silence, broken only by the ticking of the cooling engine. Blake's dad was staring at him.

Blake wiped his eyes with his hand, surprised to feel how wet they were. 'Where'd you get the lorry?' he found himself saying.

His dad just shook his head.

Still they could not find the appropriate words to say to each other.

'Lucky I noticed this place on the way to you,' his dad said.

'Lucky you were on your way to us,' Blake said, smiling.

His dad smiled too, moving a single step forward, as if to take hold of his son. But something stopped him.

Blake felt Ridley close behind him. He glanced round. The few surviving Boons and Spiders were blinking from the shadows behind the back of the truck, shivering in fear. He looked into Ridley's face, only to discover a similar dread reflected there.

'Are those things tame?' his dad asked.

Blake could not believe what he was hearing as he studied the orang-utan's fearful expression.

'Do they bite?'

'What?' Blake snapped, swinging round on him.

'You can never tell,' his dad said, 'with these things. Vanessa showed me the films and photos you took. She put them on her computer. They look like they're really tame, but wild animals never are, not really.'

Blake looked round again. But even Ridley had disappeared back into the gloom. Nothing in those images, Blake realised, could have shown the character, the real nature of the villagers.

His dad took another step towards him, to touch him. But Blake backed away. 'No,' he said. 'You don't – you still don't get it. Every since this thing began, you haven't listened to anything.'

'I know,' his dad said. 'I was wrong. But now I understand why you went back to that place. You were trying to clear your name, weren't you?'

'To begin with . . . '

'Well, now you have,' his dad smiled. 'Now I believe everything you said, everything. The monsters, the three-headed dogs—'

'Cerberus,' Blake said. 'Head Hounds.'

His dad nodded. 'Head Hounds. And white-eyed monkeys. And that terrible seal-thing, the one that looks like some kind of poor, distorted, deformed girl.'

And now, as Blake stared at his dad through the gloom, the distance between them expanded wildly. Blake was funnelled away and left standing, gasping for enough air in his lungs to begin to explain how wrong his dad was, not only about Chimera and the villagers, but about Blake himself. Blake felt the changes in him brought about by everything he had been through, shifting him away from the boy he used to be, the one who would have used the villagers to try to prove his own innocence. But now that did not matter in the least.

'We have to get away from here,' his dad was saying, from that distant point so far away. 'We have to get this lorry going and get off the moor. We have to get you home again.'

But Blake turned away. He went to the back of the truck and called out for one of those who mattered most now, calling for Chimera to come and help him with the words of explanation he could not find on his own.

Blake could hear his dad jumping back into the cab, looking for the tools to change the torn tyre on the front of the lorry.

Chimera appeared. Several other pairs of frightened eyes peered from behind her. 'What are we doing here?' she said. 'Why have we come back here?'

'*Back* here?' said Blake, glancing round. 'Why, where do you think we are?'

She went to speak, but halted at the sound of Blake's father jumping down, the clanking of a set of tools. 'We need more light,' they heard him shout. There came a snap and the electric lights all came on at once. Blake's dad appeared, lugging a hefty canvas bag.

'Why have you brought us – here, of all places?' Chimera was asking Blake's dad now.

'Here?' Mr Newton said, swinging the heavy bag. 'This is just a big farm, isn't it? Some kind of livestock centre for ... '

And then he looked up. The metal jack and wheel brace crashed to the ground.

'Why?' Chimera was still demanding of him. 'Why bring us back to this place?'

Mr Newton stepped away with his mouth dropping open at the sight and the sound of the terrible seal-girl speaking.

Blake fell away too, now that he could see in the electric lamplight through into the cages and pens surrounding them, and at the creatures kept there – cages full of heads – Hounds and

Myth Monsters, puppies, babies still, but all seemingly set in a writhing, seething mess where they had been abandoned and left to consume one another, enraged and enmaddened by growing, unbearable hunger.

Ninety

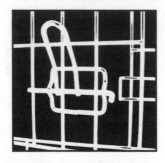

'What *is* this place?' Blake stared in horror.

He heard Chimera's voice. 'This is what I remember,' she was saying. 'This is where I came from – this is where so many of us came from.'

But Blake's dad had noticed nothing of the tangle of bitten snake-lion-goat-hound, the wretched mess of head-to-head self destruction. He was still staring open-mouthed at Chimera. 'Blake . . . ' he was stammering, 'Blake, I . . . I didn't know.'

'I'd have told you, Dad,' Blake was saying, slowly approaching the blood spattered pens, 'I'd have told you, but you were determined not to listen.'

Then his father was close by him, peering into the pens, looking at what Blake was seeing. 'I'm listening now, son. Tell me.'

Blake returned to Chimera. 'This is my father,' he said, 'and he didn't know anything about this place. Call everyone back. There's no need to be afraid.'

Chimera faltered, before making a simple sign.

Ridley appeared again, followed by the pensive Spiders and the Boons.

Blake's dad watched while his son, surrounded by villagers, placed his hand on the great orang-utan's shoulder. 'Ridley wants his picture in the papers,' Blake said. 'And that's all I wanted to do, Dad, in the end. Vanessa was right when she said everyone should know about what's been happening—'

But a scream, very high-pitched and piercing, interrupted him.

'Bonno!' Chimera said.

From outside somewhere, a huge crash. Then another, high-frequency cry of pain and anguish.

Ridley rushed to the door.

Blake went to go with him, but his dad's hand gripped him by the arm.

'Don't put yourself in any more danger,' he said.

The door opened and Ridley went out.

Blake glanced at Chimera. He shook his head, smiling, removing his dad's hand from his arm. 'All those other villagers,' he said, moving away, 'the dogs, the rabbits, the cow – I couldn't bear to lose any more.'

He went outside. Through the almost continuous wail, Blake heard his father stepping after him. Blake followed Ridley, running towards one of the nearby buildings. The door was hanging open. He saw Ridley enter, then shudder to a halt.

Blake joined him there. He stopped, just as abruptly.

The piercing cry halted as Blake's dad came in.

'Oh no,' Blake heard him say as they peered down the room at the multi-head-and-tailed, open-mouthed, mad-eyed mutations frozen solid in clear liquid.

As if suspended for ever in a moment of sheer terror, having looked into a mirror for the first time perhaps, the many-mouthed, monkey-snake and lion-goat combinations stretched out with a tiny human hand, or clawed webbed feet. One after the other, disappearing down either side of the long room the fearsome mutations morphed, in ever-more horrifying combinations. They seemed to scream silently as they were watched by their appalled audience, Blake, his father and Ridley, until another wail pierced the thickened atmosphere, one real and living, and even more terrifying than the cries petrified in formaldehyde.

Ninety-One

'It's Bonno,' said Blake, as Ridley, the first to respond, splashed through the chemical preservative awash across the floor between the folded skin and twisted claw to the other end of the horror room in the house of terror.

Blake followed him, focusing forward, avoiding the lines of eyes or the eyeless faces thrusting towards him. He could hear his father splashing close behind, as Blake trailed Ridley into the next room. He would have stopped again, he would have had to stand and stare in piled-up horror at the dissected body parts and entrails of the deceased. Only the piercing pure grief of Bonno's wail carried him through the confused cut-up mixture, the pieces of species, to where the howling bonobo crouched, his face an open mosaic of white eyes and teeth, his whole body clenched and fighting to deny the evidence of what he held in his arms.

Ridley had halted in front of Bonno, slumping to the cold wet floor. Blake moved round him to see the bonobo in his grief with his love, found at last, but lost for ever, clutched to his chest.

His soaked, falling chimpanzee face looked down. Bonno's life-mate, his love had been torn open from throat to lower stomach. Her thrown-back head stared up at him, her face still fraught with fear.

'Oh, Bonnie,' Blake said.

His dad was at his elbow, his head turning and turning, eyes darting. 'You don't need to tell me anything now,' he said. 'I've seen this – you don't need to tell me anything more.'

Bonno's cries faded away. He was looking up, at Ridley, at Blake, at Blake's dad. From one to the other the gaze of his face ranged, asking the same wordless question of each. And each in turn could do nothing to answer him.

'This is Dod,' Blake said.

Ridley put out an arm, reaching with a tentative hand to try to touch his friend the bonobo.

Bonno felt the orang-utan's fingers on his shoulder. His eyes started open, wider, whiter, wilder than ever.

He threw the dissected, flapping body at Blake. He leapt onto the laboratory benches, dragging off body parts of disparate species, a hind leg, a forepaw, a hairless monkey hand – no, a human hand!

Blake caught Bonnie's body. He watched Ridley as he lunged after Bonno. But the bonobo was too quick. He was through the door and into the other room before Blake could lay the corpse out across a bench and make a move to follow.

Blake was still placing Bonnie's arms by her side when the first crash came from the other room, accompanied by another ear-splitting scream.

As Blake rushed to the door, he saw Ridley was pushing at another of the formaldehyde tanks. The skinless and eyeless white creature inside sprawled across the floor as the glass exploded and the chemical washed over Blake's running shoes.

Bonno was springing from tank to tank, wailing, as Ridley followed him, pushing the dreadful exhibits down to smash, to swill and spill, as if the dead inhabitants were swimming for the door with all their deformed limbs.

Blake let out a cry. He too ran to one of the huge glass boxes and tried to shove it over. It was too heavy. But then Ridley was with him and the thing toppled, with a snaggle-toothed monster falling, sprawling wide, riding the wash to Blake's dad's saturated boots.

'No!' Mr Newton was shouting over the wails and roars and the cry-shouts of his son. 'Stop this!'

'Vanessa was right!' Blake heard his father's raised voice directly into his ear. 'Everyone should see. This should not be allowed to happen.'

Ridley threw another crashing container. Another wave of clear fluid chemical was washing across the floor swimming with monster-mixed abominations.

'Tell him to stop!' Blake's dad was shouting loud, close enough to be heard above the bellow-cries of bonobo and orang-utan. 'We have to leave this all intact – for everyone to see the horror.'

Blake could see that he was right. He reached for Ridley, holding him close.

Bonno was enraged still further, his pitched, pure voice beyond scream, into the realm of near glass-bursting ultra-high frequency.

'No more,' Blake mouthed at Ridley.

The world's now-fiercest bonobo gnashed towards them.

'This is evidence,' Blake's dad tried to explain, ineffectually.

Bonno leapt. He looked as if he might bite.

Ridley, pushing away from Blake, made an attempt to hold and contain his friend. But Bonno cried. He turned in frantic circles, leaping at the wretched deceased creatures apparently crying out to him.

Bonno was wild. He was lost, all his old, beautiful kindness and care gone for good. He bounced from the curved surfaces of the tanks, wailing, pulling out handfuls of his own hair. His fur, flattened by formaldehyde, looked dead. It was difficult not to see him now as one of the cross-creature abominations come back to life, raging at his makers, his destroyers, rushing out of the exit door and dashing from the factory farmyard across the open moor, seeking his revenge.

Ninety-Two

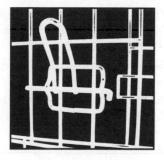

'Where is he?' Chimera was asking. 'Where's Bonno?'

Blake had had to prevent Ridley from pursuing his enmaddened friend out across the moor, with the beat of army heavy helicopter blades thumping just over the hill-top horizon.

'We had to let him go,' Blake said. 'We have to get away from here, now.'

His dad was lugging the weighted canvas bag of tools to the damaged tyre at the front of the truck.

Chimera was studying the anguish on Blake's face. 'What did you see?' she said. 'What's out there?'

Blake glanced towards his father. 'I've got to go help with the repairs.'

'No, please tell me,' Chimera said.

He looked away.

'Blake?'

He shook his head.

Chimera's eyes ranged from him to Ridley. She signed, then read the signals from his hands and from his expression. 'So,' she said, 'Dod made me here. And Dod can take me back, whenever it likes.'

'No,' said Blake. 'I won't let that happen.'

'I need some help!' his dad was calling.

Blake turned to help his father, his signals asking Ridley to go too. But the orang-utan was shaking his head madly, covering his ears.

'They're here!' Chimera said. 'They've come back.'

Blake's dad was struggling with the big lorry jack, trying to reposition it. Blake ran to help him.

From the rear of the barn a slam and crack shuddered through – then one came in from the side. The doors crashed, bulging inwards, shaking. A cloud of dust flew.

Blake and his dad were fighting to find a firm piece of ground on which to position the heavy lorry tool when from the dust cloud Ridley seemed to pour through the fuzzy air, taking the jack from Blake's hands. He threw it aside. Blake and his father could only stand back and watch.

The doors and wooden walls of the barn were under full attack now, constantly crashing, cracking, dust billowing, with the lights flashing overhead. Ridley's movements appeared staccato, like an old flickering film. He moved in a series of explosions, one frame featuring him in mid-air, full fur flying, the next and he was crouched low, fur falling. Between smash-crashes against the walls, the battered lorry's suspension creaked.

Blake and his dad, Chimera, scattered round with Boons and Spiders, all watched the film playing, showing in slow, broken motion the orang-utan as he leapt and squatted, as he heaved. They watched in wonder as the great red shoulders flexed, as the long arms strained and the front of the truck started to lift from the ground.

Reaching forward to pull at the damaged tyre, the whole weight of the loosened wheel fell against Blake's leg. But he and his dad together heaved and strained to position the spare.

Ridley let go of the wheel arch and staggered back exhausted as soon as the spare was in place.

Then the lights all went out. Blake found himself fumbling in the sudden dark, trying to locate and tighten the wheel nuts. His dad shouted something he couldn't make out. There was no sound loud enough to be heard above the wood crack and smash as the whole of the metal frame of the building shook and wobbled. Blake dropped the rest of the nuts.

But a light came on. It was not the same as before. The full beams on the lorry were suddenly breaking back through the semi-solid air.

'Get the engine started!' Blake shouted as his dad reappeared. 'Everyone on the back!' he roared towards Ridley, picking up one of the lost nuts and the wheel brace.

His dad faltered, undecided, until the doors crashed once more and a huge crack of daylight appeared.

'NOW!' screamed Blake, tightening another of the nuts. He fumbled over the next one. The wheel should have had six nuts holding it in place. Blake was tightening just the second when the doors disintegrated, flying into splinters.

As soon as the space was opened, it was filled with snarling raging faces. Lions and goats and snakes ripped forward, blocking off Blake's access to the open-backed rear of the truck.

Ninety-Three

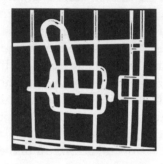

Blake dashed back to the cab and leapt in. His dad, glancing behind, was about to say something about the villagers on the back. But Blake would not allow him. 'GO!' he raged. 'Do it!' And he put his hand over his father's on the gearstick. He held that hand. Together, father and son shifted the gears and the engine screeched and knocked until Blake's dad slipped the clutch and sent them careering at break-neck acceleration straight at the back of the barn.

The wooden wall exploded outwards in a spray of flying splinters. Blake and his dad automatically shielded their eyes as the crash-through came, as they burst into the open air and the light, hitting one Myth-Monster lion head side on. The beast was sent spinning, cracking against the side of the thumping, shuddering truck.

Blake's dad was hanging grim-faced onto the steering wheel, unable to see past the splinter shower and then the crack-faced beast. Across the lumpy farmland field they trammelled, with Blake's dad spinning the wheel one way and then the other, trying to correct the slew of the vehicle across the grass.

'Look there!' Blake cried out, as soon as he saw what was coming. 'Watch out!'

Mr Newton drove his foot down as hard as he could on the brake, still trying to keep control of the steering.

The truck, twisting one way then the other, plunged front-first into the ditch, the small ravine that Blake had seen too late. The front of the lorry fell into the dip, smacking into the far bank with a soft but sickening thud, leaving the back wheels revolving in the air at top speed, with the screaming engine still driving them round and round.

Blake was not aware of shouting out. He was not conscious of his movements, the way he jammed his feet against the dashboard and held on to the frame of his seat. All these things he did without thinking because he alone saw the ditch and pictured the lorry plunging into it, thudding to a screaming stand-still with the engine left at full revs with his dad's foot jammed against the accelerator pedal.

He anticipated all this, clenching against the sudden impact, yet still had to take some time to recover from the shock of the sudden stop. The sound of the engine filled Blake's head as if it were part of him now, as if the world might never stop its wailful screeching.

'Dad,' he said, trying to dispel the sound of shriek from his ears.

Only the grind of the engine answered him.

'Dad!'

He was slumped forward, with his head against the steering wheel. Blake reached over to him.

'*Dad!*' He pulled him back. His forehead was split and bleeding. He fell, his limbs loose. The engine noise began to subside as his foot slipped from the pedal.

'Not now, Dad!' Blake shouted at him. He had turned to face his father, with his knees on the seat. 'Come on! Dad! We need you!'

Blake glanced out of the little window at the back of the cab. He could not find a single villager. All he could see was faces, forward-thrusting. Faces.

Lions. Goats. Snakes.

Ninety-Four

'Dad!' he cried. 'Dad! Oh, not now! Not now!'

His father's head was bleeding, but it didn't look too bad. Blake tried to shake him awake. He was too loose and floppy. All Blake could do was drag him out of the driver's seat and climb over him.

From the back, a scream.

'Chimera!' Blake cried out her name, while in the rear-view mirror, he saw the other, terrible Chimera, lion-roaring as the serpent lifted a Boon's body, slipping it from the piercing horns of a goat.

Blake drove his foot hard down onto the pedal he knew to be the clutch and slammed the engine into gear. He was gladdened now to remember the off-road driving he'd done with his dad.

He eased up on the clutch and down on the accelerator. The engine was engaged, he could feel the effect. But the back wheels were spinning, completely off the ground.

'Come on! Come on!' he raged at the controls. 'What can I do?'

He heard a roar, a cry, another scream of terror. In the rear-view mirror, a vast lion body was rearing up, ready to descend, driving down upon anything left alive in the back of the truck.

'No!' Blake tried to roar back at the mythical beast as it fell onto its prey, with its huge front paws slamming down against the platform.

The truck rocked with the force, with the weight of the giant bearing down on it. Blake was rising as the vehicle rocked lengthwise. His throttle foot went hard to the floor. The extra weight behind allowed the wheels to touch the ground and the lorry lurched forward.

Blake was driving the tyres into the smoking mud. But then they caught harder ground and the truck sped away so suddenly some of the few remaining villagers lost their grip and – and Blake saw the monsters bearing down on them as Boons and Spiders scrambled to escape. There was no escape, not for them. Blake had to look away, grimacing, but keeping his eyes fixed forward and his accelerator foot fully down on the floor of the truck, determined not to stop until the moor and all its monsters were far, far behind.

Ninety-Five

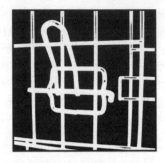

At last, Blake drove his foot down hard onto the brake pedal. He had barged his way through the twanging wire fences to the other side of the sheep enclosure. Now he sat in his driver's seat gazing along the dotted queue of camouflaged trucks and armoured cars lined up on the very edge of the Ministry of Defence ground, shaking his head slowly. 'We'll never get through,' he said.

Even as he was saying it, the other army vehicles were rumbling across the rough terrain, fanning out round the stolen truck.

'Dad,' Blake said again, without hope, 'I need you now. What shall I do?'

But the advancing vehicles were very quickly positioned in a horseshoe shape round him, with soldiers jumping from the cabs and the rear of personnel carriers, lining up to form an armed arch around Blake and his passengers.

Blake allowed himself another few moments in which to reach over and touch his dad on the forearm. There was no response.

'You in the truck!' a voice hailed through a loudspeaker. 'Get out – now!'

Blake opened the door and stuck out his head. 'It's OK!' he yelled, as much to Chimera and Ridley as to the soldiers. He clambered out, jumping down onto the springy dense grasses. Holding his hands over his head, Blake walked quickly to the back of the truck. The soldiers, he could see, were lining him up through the sights of their rifles. 'Don't shoot!'

Chimera and Ridley were huddled together as far back on the

platform as they could get. Blake stood for a while, just looking. He was still somehow expecting Boons, or a solitary Spider, to have survived. But all there was left were the two clasping one another in the corner next to the cab of the lorry, with their anxious faces, their fears flowing out towards him.

Ridley, as Blake looked back at him, could not hide his feelings. Blake saw the shame he felt, that he had made it through without saving that single Spider. Boon. Dog. Pig. Rabbit. Guinea-pig. Cow. Ridley regretted them all. His face hung. He made no sign. He did not need to.

All Blake could do, exchanging looks with Ridley, was to share his shame. He, too, was still here, with everything else he'd tried to save gone. Gone for ever. Their kind, Blake knew, would never again appear in this world.

But at least *she* was still here. At least Chimera, as she shivered in fear, was here to make people believe.

'Stay where you are,' he said, from under his still-raised hands. 'I'm just going over there to talk to some soldiers. If I just explain everything to them ... '

But his voice tailed off with Chimera and Ridley peering so intently at him. Chimera was shivering. The day was cold, but she only shook with fear. When the sun came out, her seal skin shimmered, reflecting many colours. She might appear to be cold, but Blake knew how hot she'd be feeling in the full winter sunlight. But the sight of her, the rainbow texture of her oily skin, the sheer strength and power in the almost unused muscles of her tail, her hopeful, frightened eyes – Blake felt overwhelmed by the beauty of Chimera.

'You by the lorry!' a voice was blaring over at them.

'Are we going to be safe now?' Chimera asked Blake.

The voice called again. 'Make your way towards me, now – keep your hands where I can see them clearly.'

Blake looked over at a soldier waving, gesticulating at him. 'Wait right here,' he said, looking back into Chimera's nervous face. He nodded again at Ridley. 'I won't be long,' he said.

Walking towards the line of army vehicles, Blake couldn't help noticing how the soldiers were hanging back, keeping their distance.

'I'm not armed!' Blake was calling over to them. 'It's OK – you don't understand what's been going on here.'

'That's close enough!' the soldier shouted. 'Stay exactly where you are. That is a stolen military vehicle!'

Blake looked round.

'Keep still!' the voice raged.

'But it's all right!' Blake called back. He could see movement, left and right, soldiers closing in towards the truck. He turned again.

On that moment, they were on him, diving at him, taking him down. Three, four, five of them, soldiers in full battle dress falling on top of him, forcing his face into the hard rasp of the damp grasses.

'Don't you move!' they were screaming down at him.

He still struggled. 'Listen to me! Listen to me!'

The barrel of an automatic rifle pressed into the back of his neck. 'Move, you're dead,' he heard another voice say, close to his ear.

Blake's face was forced to one side. 'Please,' he said.

'That is a stolen vehicle,' the voice said, 'and you are a terrorist.'

Blake's face was forced into the direction of his stolen truck. He could see the soldiers approaching. 'Stay away!' he tried to cry out.

He shuddered as Ridley appeared at the back of the platform.

'Don't you move!' the soldiers were screaming.

'It's some kind of ape!' some other soldiers were calling back to them. 'Some kind of gorilla!'

'Ridley!' Blake cried out. 'Stay there! Keep still! Don't move!'

He could see Ridley looking over at him. And he could see the soldiers looking past Ridley, stepping away, with *that* expression on their faces. Blake knew then that he had looked like that the first time he had seen Chimera.

'It's all right!' he tried to shout over at the soldiers.

But they were backing away as Chimera was trying to hide her body from their horror-struck faces. The soldiers were as afraid as she was, raising their weapons as Ridley leapt to the ground, running at them with his arms out, roaring.

'What *is* that thing?' Blake heard them shouting.

'There's something here!' one was calling over to the soldiers holding Blake.

'It's all right!' Blake was struggling to break free.

'There's something over here!'

'Some kind of creature!'

'No!' Blake cried out. 'Don't call her that!'

Ridley was raging back and forth between Chimera on the back of the platform and the rifles ranged against them.

'What the hell is it?' Blake could hear the fear in the questions of the armed guard.

'It's all right!' Blake was trying to answer them.

Ridley was every moment more agitated as Chimera backed away, more and more afraid.

'What the hell is it?'

'Some kind of – it's some kind of monster!'

Ninety-Six

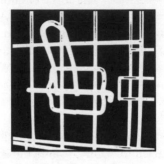

A gun went off. One bullet was all it took. The situation changed from shouts to shots. The soldiers dispersed, and Blake was up and tearing across the rough grasses and the heather, with guns going off.

Ridley was all roar now, lunging forward, lashing out at gun barrels, dashing the firearms from the shoulders of frightened soldiers. His flying fur made him appear almost twice his actual size. He was everywhere, protecting Chimera as she screamed from her corner at the far end of the lorry platform.

Blake dashed up in a rage like Ridley's, making himself bigger than he really was, diving into the side of one armed man as he aimed at the monsters he saw before him. Blake knocked him to the ground. The soldier's ear was torn and bleeding. Blake ran at the next man.

Maybe it was the sound of gunfire, or the orang-utan roars and the soldiers' shouts that managed to revive Blake's dad, but the lorry had started up, swinging round and bouncing to a halt. 'On the back!' he was yelling, with his still-dazed face hanging out of the open window. 'Get on the back!'

Blake snatched up a rifle and fired, once, into the air. He threw it down again. Ridley was right behind him, picking Blake up and throwing him onto the back of the truck.

Blake found himself suddenly raised above the ground and heaped onto the hard wooden platform. Blue smoke coughed from the exhaust as the engine roared under them. Ridley was turning, swirling like a red whirlwind against the force of the oncoming troops.

'Ridley!' Blake screamed. The lorry engine was engaged and they were starting forward with a jerk. 'Ridley! *Now!*'

They were moving away from the ragged semi-circle of the army cordon, with soldiers shouting and running, or jumping back into the cabs and driving seats of their vehicles.

'Ridley!' Blake raged.

From behind him, the same word: 'Ridley!' Chimera screamed for him.

'Come on!' Blake was shouting to him as Ridley finally twisted and turned and started to swing towards the accelerating truck.

The other army lorries were on the move, pursuing them. But Blake saw only the wide orang-utan face, watching Ridley leaping along behind the moving platform. Blake's dad was shifting gears, stepping up the speed. He couldn't have known Ridley had not yet swung far enough, that his son was anchoring himself by gripping onto one of the side slats, holding out his other hand.

'Come on, Ridley!' His arm stretched.

Chimera had come back to hold Blake, her arms going round his waist. She was clinging onto him. He was glad to feel her there.

Blake touched Ridley's warm dry fingers with his own. They tried to grip one another.

Behind Ridley, Blake was aware of the soldiers, running, of lorries, accelerating.

'Do it, Ridley!' he roared down into Ridley's face. Their eyes were locked. 'Come on! You have to!'

And Ridley did. He somehow found the extra strength to leap forward and grip Blake by the wrist, almost wrenching his arm out of its socket. Without Chimera's extra weight, Blake would never have been able to keep hold. He would have been dragged off. As it was, his shoulder felt as if it were being ripped apart, with Ridley hanging off the back of the truck, one hand round Blake's wrist, his feet gripping the metal edge of the platform.

Blake heaved back. Ridley weighed – he did not know how much, but at least three times as much as Blake. But Blake clenched his teeth and hauled until Ridley's other hand caught hold of the metal upright at the end of the platform and he held on.

Ridley pulled himself up, standing on the very back of the truck as Blake collapsed, he and Chimera falling on top of each other. Over them, Ridley stood and let out a roar of victory, with his arms outstretched. He looked bigger than ever, with his hands up, his fur flying in the ever-strengthening wind.

And then he stopped, as if shocked. His face had changed. He looked down at Blake, at Chimera.

They saw the change in him before they heard the shot. And then they heard the shot.

Ninety-Seven

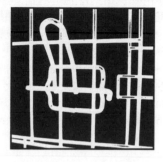

It felt like a long time. Blake seemed to be somehow waiting, with fears spiralling in at him, tumbling all at once, every one more terrifying than the last.

'Oh, no!' he thought he heard Chimera's voice, but it might have been another horror-thought arriving.

Ridley was looking at him intently. Too intently. Blake stared back at him, taking on his look, waiting, somehow, for this time to end.

'Oh, no!' he did hear Chimera say.

Ridley was lowering himself, sitting slowly, still exchanging the long, unbroken look with Blake. He just sat down on the very back edge of the vehicle, with another kind of look coming into his eyes. His mouth came open slightly.

'Ridley?' Blake said. 'Ridley?'

Blake stood, reaching for him.

'Oh, no!' Chimera said, again, from behind him.

He reached out. Ridley's hand started to move. He was trying to raise his arm, to take Blake's hand.

'Ridley! No!'

And the great orang-utan fell backwards from the shifting, bouncing truck, hitting the ground hard in a final flurry of deep red, blood-reddened fur.

'Ridley!' Chimera was screaming. 'Not you, Ridley! Oh no! Ridley – NO!'

But Blake, standing at the back of the bouncing vehicle, holding on with one hand, the other still reaching out, had to watch the soldiers running up to the dead red body, firing more bullets into it. More bullets. More and more bullets.

Blake winced and cringed with every new hit. They were on top of what had been Ridley, firing from point-blank range. Blake shuddered with the shock of every hit. But Ridley felt nothing now.

'He's gone,' Blake said, as if to Chimera. His words were taken away on the wind.

Chimera's cries were blown back to him. 'Not Ridley! Please – oh – please!'

'They've murdered him!' Blake said. 'Those people – people like me – not monsters – people like me, Chimera! They've murdered Ridley!'

He crouched by her. She had to hold onto him. There was nothing else, no one left to cling to. 'I'm sorry,' he said, to her. 'I'm so sorry,' speaking as if to them all, to Ridley and every other missing village being.

Then another shot sounded out across the moor. And then another.

Ninety-Eight

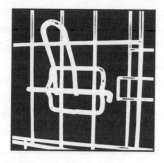

'I'm going to find a way off the moor!' Blake's dad was yelling out of his window.

Blake was standing on the back straining to hear, with Chimera holding hard round his waist. Ridley's body had disappeared into the far distance, surrounded by his attackers, his murderers.

'Ridley!' Chimera was crying. 'Oh – what am I going to do without Ridley?'

'My dad's going to get us out of here!' Blake was shouting at her. 'Chimera, listen to me – Ridley would never forgive me if anything happened to you. Focus on what we have to do. Ridley wouldn't want you to—'

But then some kind of object seemed to thump against the underside of the lorry, lifting Blake and Chimera, throwing them back down. The back of the platform slewed wildly to one side, threatening to slide them both straight off.

Blake managed to keep hold of one of the metal slats at the side. Chimera was still clinging to him.

'Dad!' he shrieked.

Blake tried to stand. The lorry was listing drunkenly now, vibrating wildly down the other side of the hill. At first, Blake had thought that one of the cannons on the armoured cars had blasted them with a shell, hitting their underside. But as he looked through the little window at the fight his dad was having with the steering, he knew that the front wheel he'd fixed so inadequately back there in the barn, had worked its way loose. And it was about to fall off.

Skidding and sliding, still gathering speed, the juddering and trembling felt as if the lorry was coming to bits. Blake could no longer hold onto the metal. He fell with Chimera again. They felt the world tipping wildly to one side. Everything was screeching, vibrating, screaming.

The juddering ended with a bang like an explosion at the front of the truck and a blanket of mud was flung out. The metal sides screeched as the whole truck tipped and flew over onto its side.

Everything flew. For what seemed like a long, long time, Blake turned inside a tumble of hillsides and skies, metal and mud, his own shouts and Chimera's screams. Everything revolved around him as he watched the bend and grind of metal and shattered glass glittering in a mighty skein of flying, flopping mud.

Ninety-Nine

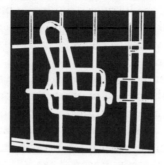

The spinning world spiralled inwards, collapsing to a grinding halt with a final squeal of metal and a flop and splat of grassy mud. At that pinpoint in time, everything went suddenly still, and so very silent.

Blake waited, to be certain the new stillness and silence were real and not just happening inside him. But then a sound ended it. Chimera called him, her voice breaking through from somewhere seemingly much further away.

The side-slats of the lorry were above him as Blake disentangled himself from the twisted wreckage of metal and mud supporting his back. He quickly inspected the platform floor that now stood as a wall facing him.

'Blake!' Chimera's voice came through again.

Crawling carefully across the broken metal slats Blake made it to the muddied, scarred hillside from the side-down lorry with the crushed cabin up in front.

Chimera had slipped out, Blake could see, in the spinning slide as the truck turned over down the decline of the hill. She had flown out and slapped down, sliding from the crashing vehicle on the slither of her strong shiny tail. There she sat, unharmed, watching Blake as he emerged, also unscathed, with a look of intense concern on her face. 'Your father!' she was pointing towards the front of the truck.

Only now did Blake see how damaged, how crushed the driver's cabin was. He ran across the mud, crunching over the jewels of broken glass underfoot.

The roof of the cabin had been pushed down as the mud and undersoil had piled up against the push of the fallen vehicle. A great heap of dirt had gathered, collapsing the roof further and further down into the space that had contained the driver.

'Dad!' Blake cried, leaping onto the side door that now faced the sky. He tugged at the handle. 'Dad!' he called again, peering through the rough slot that was once the driver's side window.

'I'm all right,' he heard a voice contained inside. 'I'm fine.'

His dad's voice made it through the small gap, but included another element that Blake did not like to hear. 'You're hurt!' Blake called though, just able to see his father now, trapped between two buckled seats, with his arm bleeding and held strangely backwards, at a very unnatural angle. 'Dad – your arm!'

'I don't think it's broken.' The voice that came through was pained, while trying to sound strong.

Blake couldn't help but notice the greenish pallor of the face peering out at him.

'I think it's been dislocated – but I'm all right.'

The door would not give as Blake heaved against it. 'I'll get you out,' he called through the gap.

As he said it, the sound of an explosion boomed across the hilltops. In the direction from which they had come, a huge billow of black smoke rose against the sky. Another missile struck and thumped and the cloud mushroomed much faster and harder.

'What is it?' Mr Newton was shouting out to his son. 'What's going on?'

Blake took a quick glance at the look on Chimera's face. 'They're bombing Dod,' he said, hoping that she might be made happier by that fact.

But the missiles were falling too close to Chimera to allow her, or Blake, any real comfort.

'They're destroying everything,' he spoke close to the gap in the crushed door. 'They're getting rid of all the evidence.'

He looked back at Chimera again. 'She's all that's left,' he said, with his mouth at the window, as if to keep a secret with his dad.

'Keep going,' his dad hissed back, keeping the confidence with his son. 'Down into the valley.'

Blake rattled at the door handle again. 'I can't just leave you here. I've got to get you out.'

'Go!' his dad yelled. 'I'll be fine. They'll be on their way here soon. Get her away. You have to, Blake.'

'But Dad, I—'

'Just do it, son. You were right to come back, to try to do something about what you saw. Now see it through. Look down into the valley. It's your only chance. I'm proud of you, son – this is another race, and you're in the lead, at the moment. I want to see you win, I do, more than ever.'

One Hundred

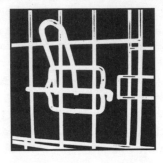

He could see it running through the valley like a finishing tape. 'The River Moor!' he announced through gritted teeth.

Blake was assisting Chimera dragging herself down the hill, straining to lift her over a fence, giving up, kicking a gap through for her. She was silent now, apart from her deep-voice gasps of exasperation as she squirmed and slapped her winding way over the grass towards the trees.

'We have to get to cover,' Blake was trying to urge her along, sweating, resisting his own impatience. 'Be careful across this wire. Take your time,' he said, when all he really wanted to do was to shout at her to Hurry! Hurry! Hurry!

He kept looking back to see if the soldiers had made it up and over the hill yet, not wanting to see them while at the same time, anxious for them to help his dad. He glanced around again, watching for helicopters, for blue suits. But the bombardment over the horizon had continued for some time as Blake slid Chimera away, pulling her along, pushing her up the sides of hillocks, falling over her, toiling, labouring to make the ribbon of the distant river.

At last they were crashing through bushes into the trees on the approach to the water's edge. A thin line of camouflaged vehicles appeared, trundling across the top of the hill towards the tipped-over truck.

'Here,' Blake guided Chimera across the leaf-mould of the

woods now, pointing away from the advancing army between the trees at the fast-flowing wintertime waters.

'The River Moor!' he exclaimed, running the last few yards. He turned back to Chimera with an expression of triumph. 'We made it!'

'Made it?' she said, looking around. 'What have we made?'

'We've made it here,' he pointed at the dark rush of the water. 'The river. This will take us away. This is where my dad was trying to bring us.'

Overhead, giant helicopter blades chopped the air, whipping the uppermost bare branches of the trees into a frenzy. It passed over, then was gone.

'Come on,' Blake said, helping Chimera move further forward. 'Now we can really move.'

'What do you mean – move, how?'

Blake was trying to lead her into the shallows, but Chimera was stalling, sticking to the ground with the solidity of her heavy tail. 'Come on,' Blake assured her, 'if you swim and I run, we can—'

'Swim?' she said. Her horrified face was fixed on the shifting surface of the fast waters. 'You mean . . . go in there?'

'Yes!' he snapped, marching up to the very edge. He could hear the engines now, hammering down the hill towards the woods. 'I mean . . . yes, swim!'

'Is this the sea?'

'No. I told you, it's the river. Now, if you'd just go in the water—'

But she turned in panic and started to flap back the way they had come.

Blake ran to her. 'What are you doing? You can't go up there. Look,' he pointed to the rapidly advancing vehicles.

'I can't go in there!' she pointed with a shaking forefinger.

For all the danger they had faced, Blake had never seen such dread and panic in Chimera's eyes. 'But I thought,' he said, 'I thought you were made for this, for the water. You *were* made for this! Look at you. Chimera, you don't know what you can do.'

'Neither do you!'

'But your tail – your webbed hands! I *do* know, Chimera.'

'And so do I!' she snapped. 'I know I'm not going in there, no matter what you say.' She was staring at him with a look of fear-fuelled defiance.

'OK!' Blake cried. 'OK. We'll just stay here then, shall we?'

Chimera looked again at the river. She was almost solid with fear.

'OK!' Blake said again. 'Right, come on. We follow the river downstream anyway. It'll just be a whole, whole lot slower.'

'I'm sorry,' Chimera said, glancing away from the water again.

'It's doesn't matter,' he said, peering through the trees, 'I think I have a plan. Over there, look, on the bank.'

There was a little house with a garden that sloped down to the water's edge. On the lawn, a line hung with clothes. Moored nearby, a tiny boat, a skiff with a little outboard motor.

Blake ran over, tugging a sheet from the washing line. 'Quickly!' he called, pulling at the rope that held the boat to the bank. Chimera thumped along beside him. 'In the boat!' he cried, as a shout came from the edge of the woods behind them.

Soldiers were streaming through the trees towards them.

Blake was heaving the heavy seal-tail into the boat, throwing the sheet from the washing line over Chimera's body. He tugged at the string on the outboard motor.

It banged into life with a puff of blue smoke as the first of the soldiers, the man with the torn ear, arrived on the bank, reaching out and almost toppling over into the river.

Blake stared back at him as he turned the throttle control and drove the little boat very quickly downstream, leaving the soldiers gathering on the bank behind, with their officer ordering them to put down their firearms while straining, desperately, to get a better look at Chimera again.

One Hundred-and-One

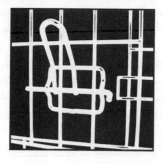

'After my mum died,' Blake said, breathing easily for the first time in a long while, beginning to enjoy steering the skiff downstream, 'my dad and me, we rowed a boat for miles on this river.'

'Why?' said Chimera, staring over the side as at something terrifying.

'It was like,' Blake said, remembering how he had felt that day, 'as my dad said, it was the next stage of the journey. As if we'd come from somewhere upstream originally, and the river was just taking us where we were always going to go. But we had to feel that we were still going there together, and it was a place worth going to ... somewhere good.'

Chimera was looking at him then. 'Just like we are, Blake,' she said. 'Like us, coming from up there,' she turned and pointed, 'where Dod was. That's where we've come from, Blake, isn't it?'

'Yes,' he said, noticing how she, always too warm, had pushed the sheet from her body and most of her tail.

'And that's where we're going to,' Chimera's pointing finger swept from up to downstream, towards the town of Moormouth on the estuary. More and more houses were gathering on the banks of the river. 'It's somewhere worth going to, Blake, isn't it? Somewhere good?'

But Blake was remembering the reaction of the soldiers on the moor, the horror and fear they had expressed on seeing Chimera's seal skin and her cross-species lower body.

'Dod's gone,' Chimera was reiterating, looking for comfort and reassurance, 'and this is a good place to go, isn't it, Blake?'

His mind was fixed on the soldiers' faces, at the shots they'd fired at the shifting platform of the accelerating lorry, hitting Ridley, ending him. And all along the banks now, as Blake covered Chimera with the stolen sheet, near-familiar faces stared with similar expressions, every one of them ready to be horrified, as Blake was, on first sight of a morphed, misshapen seal-girl.

'Blake?' she was saying, desperate to receive a kind word in return as she looked over at the houses, the buildings ascending the hill to the Naval College like the crown on the head of the whole town. 'It is good, isn't it?'

Chimera never received the answer she was looking for. Blake, struggling to find the right thing to say to her, said nothing. But he would not have been heard anyway, above the sudden rotor-blade burst of noise from the three helicopters thumping downstream behind them and the flotilla of military dinghies bouncing into view round the car ferry at the sea-end of the estuary town.

Blake opened the engine control to full throttle, driving between the boats for the quayside, packed with everyday, non-uniform-wearing people. 'Stay covered,' Blake was instructing Chimera as she shifted under the slipping sheet. 'Keep your tail out of sight.'

The helicopters were homing in, the high-powered inflatables forming a tighter and tighter semicircle from which there was now no escape.

The tide must have been out as the top of the quay was over Blake's head as he stood in the skiff. He gripped a ladder fixed to the side. A crowd had quickly gathered above him at the sight of the military flying overhead and floating behind.

'Don't let them see you,' Blake looked round to say to Chimera. 'Not just yet.'

'I can't climb that,' Chimera said, peering up and up the ladder, rung by rung. 'Don't go without me, Blake. Blake – don't leave me!'

'I won't,' he was about to say. He didn't get that far. Blake found himself gripped by the back of his jacket and dragged upwards.

Suddenly all Blake could see was a face thrust into his own, the one with the plaster over the bridge of its nose where it had been bitten by a frantic, white-eyed bonobo chimpanzee.

'We meet again, at last.' The face above the ministry-blue suit was peering over the edge. It smiled. 'And you had the common decency to keep the abomination covered. Thank you so very, very much for your kind co-operation.'

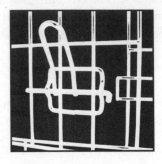

Soldiers took him by the arms as the blue-suited man from the ministry leered into Blake's face. 'You've done remarkably well, lad,' he smiled, 'I'll say that for you. What a game, eh?'

He turned to peer over the side again at Chimera cowering below under the cover of her thin sheet.

'But now it's game over. Nice try, but you lose. Get those people back! We need to get an ambulance in here. There's a paraplegic down there who needs our help.' He turned his full concentration back onto Blake. 'Isn't that right, lad – a girl with no legs, who needs us to take care of her?' He glanced down again, returning with a slippery smile. 'And we will take good care of her, Blake Newton, on that you can rely.'

'I'm still going to tell everyone what happened here,' Blake said.

'Oh, really? And how is your battle against drug addiction going?'

'But my dad knows—'

'Oh yes, your dad. You're quite a little family unit, aren't you? The newspapers, the people will be bound to believe you and your dad, of course they will. A convicted drugs thief, the son of a drunkard, with tales of horrid monsters coming to get him.'

'I've got photos.'

The man shook his head slowly, smiling. 'No. No you haven't. You don't even have that abomination down there you're so taken with. You have nothing.'

'You've destroyed them all.'

'They destroyed themselves.'

'Not Ridley. Not Chimera. Or Bonnie the bonobo.'

'Apes, seals and monkeys. Animals are destroyed in experiments every day for the sake of mankind. We kill a few beasts, open up the odd chimpanzee, there's nothing wrong with that . . . '

Blake caught the merest glimpse before the hit came. The man was talking about murdering monkeys when something dropped from the high roof over the little road. It sprang from the guttering where it must have been squatting, watching, listening, waiting, and launched itself, arms out, mouth fully open.

'. . . there's nothing wrong with that—' he had been saying, when it thumped home, the leaper from the roof, fixing right round the man's head with arms and tight legs, flashing white eyes full of hate and champing teeth.

'Bonno!' Blake just managed to cry.

The man, his head and face completely encased by bonobo, flew into a spin as the soldiers round him stepped away in alarm. The ministry man staggered backwards, his distressed cries muffled as the chimpanzee bit harder into him. One of his feet slipped over the edge. The man reached out and caught Blake by the collar and they fell from the quayside towards the little boat on which Chimera was hiding herself beneath a single flimsy sheet.

One Hundred-and-Three

Chimera tried to catch hold of Blake. She screamed as together they tumbled from the tilting, rocking skiff into the breathless cold of the river. Blake splashed to the surface almost immediately, gaping for air. For a moment or two he was aware of the sodden ministry blue suit thrashing against the gnashing bonobo chimpanzee clamped about his head.

Blake just saw the man and the monkey sinking into the water, continuing the fight for life, the struggle for revenge. Soldiers were dropping into the river from above, attempting to save the ministry man as he and his attacker disappeared beneath the surface. None of them reached him in time.

The sudden cold was paralysing. It shocked every sense, denying movement to the muscles. Blake went down, aware of the waterlogged blue suit sinking more quickly than he was. He watched the man turning limply in the current, his head and face wrapped, ripped in vengeance by the crazed and changed bonobo.

Their last lungfuls came rolling towards him, bubbles that flew away upwards. Blake followed them up and up again.

He burst out onto the surface of the river, gasping and gagging, colder than he could ever have imagined. It was like being squeezed, restricted by water as his heat and energy evaporated at a horrifying rate.

He was going down again. His legs and his arms would not move now. Blake's *eyes* were cold. He sank, stone solid on the sudden drowning moment. So stiff a hardened body with such fused, metallic limbs, was never going to stay on the surface for more than a few moments.

Blake found himself smiling up at the face of the sun. It seemed to smile back and reach down to him, enfolding him in its extended limbs of light. He felt himself lifted, held. Blake found himself rising, floating upwards into the light and the heat, back into his life. He re-emerged, coughing out the water air bubbles he had inhaled.

Chimera, for ever so cold to the touch, was warm as she held Blake in the water. She swam, for the first time in her life. Her tail moved in the way it had always, always wanted. She was built for this, although she had not known it.

She *should* have been in the water all her life. Now Chimera understood this. Blake could feel her gratified acceptance in the way she moved, the heat she generated, the warm air she was able to blow into his lungs to replace his last lost deep breath. Chimera's mermaid breath had always been far deeper than Blake's deepest.

Exploding onto the surface of the fast-flowing river with Blake cradled in her arms, she twisted under and round him as he coughed and gasped and coughed again. She was laughing. 'This is what you meant by swimming,' she was saying, almost deliriously.

Blake's body was soaking up her warmth, consuming it. She was so strong under him, holding him so powerfully, with the two of them together in the same spot, stationary as the swift current slipped past.

But the dinghies were turning, the men on board pointing them out. Blake recognised the young soldier with the torn ear. 'Chimera,' he spluttered, 'get away.'

As she continuously changed her body position against eddies in the current, Blake was reminded of a kestrel – she trod water as that little bird of prey rode the wind. It was as effortless, as absolute, as if she and he were wallowing in a stagnant pond rather than against a powerfully flowing stream.

'You were made for this,' Blake said.

'Don't move!' the soldier shouted to him. 'Stay right where you are!'

'You just follow the current now, Chimera,' Blake shivered. 'The sea – it's down there,' he said through clashing teeth, watching the motorised military dinghies bouncing against the current towards them.

She was still holding him. It was easy for her. The small flotilla of blow-up boats surged forward in a ragged line. But still Chimera did not move. She was staring at Blake.

'Go,' he said softly. 'To the sea. The sea, Chimera.'

'We're going together,' she said, peering downstream. 'Take a breath,' she said. 'And make it deep.'

And with that, they were dipping down without a splash, with Chimera's tail driving them rapidly to the bottom, both still looking at each other. Chimera's face in front of Blake's was fading out in the murky muddiness of the deeper water. It was colder down there. His body, still held close to hers, was wracked with painful shivers.

Blake lost sight of her then. So close together, they were in a cloud flipped up from the bottom of the river by a whale-tail. The force forwards, following the flow, was so fast Blake exhaled in astonishment.

All this Blake felt as his heart picked up pace, and up again. Moving downstream into the estuary, they were fish-fast, easily outrunning any clumsy inflatable power boats. The floating army were left behind, a long way. The river was very deep here, but Chimera kept them skimming along the muddy bottom. Blake was just holding his breath, while Chimera was doing something much cleverer with hers – storing it in some secret way, putting it in pockets in her locked lungs for use much later on.

Blake's head was going from side to side. He was wracked with cold, his ears thudding with water pressure and the need to breathe. He tried to shout out but his voice was left a long way behind in bubbles of spent oxygen.

Chimera was immensely, astonishingly powerful. He had never realised, always thinking himself the stronger. Maybe he was, with her waddling next to him on dry land. But here – here he was going to die in her arms, of breathing water. He was – he was going to – going to—

PART FOUR

The Whole Wide World

One Hundred-and-Four

The waters closed over him, enfolding and gently holding him. As if a person's perfect seal-tail propelled him through the current, Blake felt the flow, the wash of the ebbing tide that left him stranded, face up. He stared at the light. He was not cold, but rather too warm, like Chimera herself. He had, perhaps, become more like her, swimming by her side in the open, endless sea.

But under him now, the solid strand of a beach supported his back. The light overhead dried him out in an instant and he saw a ceiling interrupting his view of the sky, a strip light fixed where the sun should have been.

A face appeared. 'Are you awake?'

Blake recognised her. He just wasn't expecting to see her here – not here, like this, today.

'I'll go and fetch the nurse,' Vanessa's face was saying to him.

He glanced to the side. Out of the window, a bare winter tree stood against the cloudy grey of the sky. 'Wait!' Blake said, reaching out for her.

Vanessa, twitching almost uncontrollably, came back and took Blake's hand. 'How are you feeling?' she asked.

Blake took a breath. All round him, the hospital room gathered, containing him too closely. The sea was not here, anywhere. 'What happened?' he said.

'You're safe now,' Vanessa smiled. 'I'll just go and tell—'

'How am I here?' Blake started to sit up. 'Who brought me?'

Vanessa looked alarmed at Blake's agitation. She reached out, before Blake could stop her, and she pressed the emergency attention button on the wall behind.

Blake was upright in bed, looking about wide eyed, clasping Vanessa's thin hand. 'Tell me what happened!'

She held him back as tightly. 'Blake, I don't know what happened.'

'Who – who brought me here?'

'A soldier, I think. He was here earlier, to see how you are.'

Blake stared into her face. 'With a torn ear?'

'What?'

'His ear – his left ear was cut. Was it?'

'He did have a dressing on his ear, yes. He said he'd taken you out of the sea.'

Blake collapsed back. 'Then I did nothing!' he said. He turned violently onto his side, letting go of Vanessa's hand. 'Nothing!' He stared back at her over his shoulder. 'All of them – every single one, gone!'

Tears were all over his face.

'I'll go and fetch your dad,' Vanessa looked afraid.

Blake was wild. He turned in bed again. 'They destroyed them all!' he said, almost shouting. 'What did I do? I took them out into the world.'

'Your dad's just having his dressings changed,' Vanessa was saying at the door, with a nurse appearing by her side. 'I'll go and get him for you.'

The nurse, advancing across the room, was reaching for Blake's wrist.

He flicked his arm away, turning from her. 'All gone!' he said.

'Just a moment!' the nurse took hold of him, as Blake was about to get out of bed. 'Calm down, young man!'

'I need to know!' he shouted. 'Where's that soldier? I need to know what they did with her!'

The nurse ran to the door, blocking Blake's exit. A man appeared, a porter in green trousers and top.

'What are you?' Blake's eyes were crazed. 'A Greencoat, are you? What is this place? Another Dod?'

'Help me get him back into bed,' the nurse instructed the man. Another green porter appeared. They were forcing Blake backwards as he fought to make it to the door.

'Stop!' a voice rang out.

Blake broke free and ran into his dad's arms, one of which was in a sling. His dad was wincing in pain, but still holding hard onto his son. 'Come on,' he said, gently. 'Back into bed, Blake. Come on, my boy.'

'But they got them all.' Blake was crying.

His dad was limping, with one of his ankles in a plaster cast.

Blake sat on the bed. 'You're hurt,' he said, noticing his father's dressings.

The nurse and the two orderlies stood away.

'I'm OK,' Blake's dad smiled and nodded at the medical staff. 'I'm fine, if you are. Get back into bed, Blake.'

A doctor appeared, along with another nurse carrying a tray of medications and a hypodermic syringe. 'How are you now, Blake?' the doctor approached.

Blake backed away at the sight of the nurse preparing the syringe. 'Don't let them, Dad.'

'It's only a sedative,' the doctor said, speaking to Blake's father. 'It will help him rest.'

'I don't need to rest!'

His dad turned to him.

Vanessa was looking in from outside.

His dad was still smiling. He placed his hands on Blake's shoulders. 'It's going to be all right,' he said.

'But they took her. The soldier with his ear ripped on the moor, he came here and he—'

'He came to tell you something,' his dad said. He leaned in closer, closer still. He was whispering directly into Blake's ear. 'He came to tell you that it's all over. Everything that was out there is gone – destroyed. The charges against you, all of them, will be dropped. A statement's already been prepared by the police to be issued to the press.'

Blake tensed. He wanted to shout out but his father's grip tightened on his shoulders. 'I don't care about that,' he managed to whisper. 'I only care about ...'

'Chimera went back,' his dad interrupted. 'She brought you in to them. She knew you'd die otherwise. She did it for you, Blake, after everything you did for her.'

They were looking at each other again. Once more, his father leaned in.

'She's happy now,' Blake heard him whisper. 'You did it, my son. She's free.'

Blake's tension grew. 'They let her go?'

'That captain ... he watched her swim away. He said, he told me to tell you that he'd never seen anything like it, anything so beautiful as Chimera swimming off into the distance. She was jumping clean out of the water.'

'It was everything she'd ever dreamed of,' Blake breathed, letting go. He let his dad ease him back into bed.

'Everything she'd ever dreamed of,' his dad said, waving away the hypodermic-wielding doctor and the nurses and their muscled porters, 'and you made it happen for her, my boy.'

As his dad turned away to speak to the doctor, Blake lay back. Tears were streaming from his eyes. He blinked, and Vanessa was there, close to him.

'Don't say anything,' she whispered. 'I've saved the pictures, all the images, backed up on the Net. They're all there.'

Blake almost broke down. But his dad was back, standing next to Vanessa. 'I'm never going to let her go, Dad,' he whispered. 'I'm never going to forget what they did to them, to all the villagers. I'm going to understand it,' he said, glancing up at Vanessa, 'all of it – the science, everything. Chimera's never, never going to let me stop asking questions now.'

His dad was looking at him with that expression on his face, as if Blake had just won the race of his life. Vanessa had stepped back, smiling from just inside the door. She knew that look.

But Blake knew his race was only just beginning. 'I'll never stop now,' he whispered, 'never give in to them. Chimera's free! I can – see her – I can really see her!'

'Just like your mum can see you,' his dad said.

Blake closed his eyes. He could picture Chimera better that way, as if he were still there with her as she jumped, watching her lithe strong body rise and flex and fall, watching her alive in the whole wide world of the sea as she had never been before, laughing and calling to him, asking him never to forget, before waving him goodbye.

John Brindley lives with his wife in the south-east of England, and has two grown-up children. He enjoys taking long walks in the countryside around his home and listening to all types of music. John trains and plays squash to keep fit and rides a mountain bike when the weather's good.

About his writing, John says:

'For as long as I can remember, one of my main interests, besides literature, has been science. My books *The Rule of Claw* and *City of Screams* are set in this world but where the scientific laws of evolution are running wild.

'*Legend* continues in that vein, exploiting my fascination with the natural processes that made us and the changes that could be made *in* us – either through those processes or by human interference.

'The science in my books, along with the changes that it brings, is based on what is actually happening here and now. The changes that I write about haven't come about . . . at least, not yet.'